An Inveterate Mountie

Adventures of the First Woman Mountie. Book 16

LAURIE SCHRAMM

This book is a work of historical fiction, set in the early 1980s. Although most of the historical references are accurate, a few are not, and names, characters, places, and incidents are either the product of the author's imagination or are used fictitiously. Any resemblance to actual persons, living or dead is entirely coincidental.

Print ISBN: 978-1-0690565-6-6
ePub ISBN: 978-1-0690565-7-3

Laurie Schramm

inveterate

adjective: having a long-established, ingrained habit

The Canadian Oxford Dictionary, Oxford University Press, 1998

Laurie Schramm

DEDICATION

To Dr. Joe Muldoon, Ph.D., M.B.A., B.Sc., with whom I made so many enjoyable trips to the fascinating, real-life Gunnar Mine, Mill, and Townsite on the north shore of Lake Athabasca.

Laurie Schramm

CONTENTS

Laurie Schramm

ACKNOWLEDGMENTS

I am extremely grateful to the growing number of friendly readers that that have provided encouragement, comments, and suggestions based on drafts of these books: Ann Marie, Katherine, Victoria, William, Dawson, Al, Jayme, Karen M., and Ernie.

Special thanks also to five real-life veterans of the RCMP, all of whom have supplemented their encouragement with background, advice, and factual reference materials on the Force: Chief Superintendent William Schramm (Ret.), who also kindly allowed my main character to borrow his Regimental Number, Assistant Commissioner Dawson Hovey (Ret.), Deputy Commissioner Peter German, KC, Ph.D. (Ret.), Constable Karen Frost (Ret., one of the trailblazing women Mounties who joined-up when women represented only 2% of the total uniformed complement), and especially Staff Sergeant Al Lund (Ret., author of *Mounties on the Cover* and probably the world's leading authority on Mountie fiction).

Laurie Schramm

LIST OF CHARACTERS
(IN ORDER OF APPEARANCE)

- Harland Walker, a United States Senator
- Dr. Ernst Wildersbach, owner of Athabasca Outfitters
- Lisa, a radiation-therapy technician
- Robert Johnson, a mysterious American
- Ben Delorme, a fly-in fishing-camp guide
- Sergeant Alexandra (Alex) Houston, RCMP Security Service
- Silver, an Alaskan Malamute; Alex's police-service-dog partner
- Major Donald (Don) Harrison, Military Intelligence, Canadian Armed Forces
- Deputy Commissioner George MacLeod, RCMP Security Service
- Rear-Admiral Peter White, head of the Canadian Forces Security Branch
- Staff Sergeant Avery Blunt, RCMP Security Service
- Special Agent Vivian Rule, FBI
- Richard Cooper, CIA operative
- Alistair Hughes, camp cook, Athabasca Outfitters
- Dexter Sherman, a computer consultant and sometime hacker

ACRONYMS AND ABBREVIATIONS

AECL	Atomic Energy of Canada Limited
AI	Artificial Intelligence
CFB	Canadian Forces Base
CIA	U.S. Central Intelligence Agency
CPIC	Canadian Police Information Centre
ESP	Extra-sensory perception
FBI	U.S. Federal Bureau of Investigation
HQ	Headquarters
MI6	British Secret Intelligence Service
RCAF	Royal Canadian Air Force
RCMP	Royal Canadian Mounted Police
SUV	Sport Utility Vehicle
U of A	University of Alberta
WATS	Wide Area Telephone Service

CODE WORDS

Sparrow	The first CIA operative, Robert Johnson
Hawk	Captured or killed
Cat	Richard Cooper
Mouse	Vivian Rule
Dog	Alex Houston
Guns	Don Harrison
Turtle	Dexter Sherman

1 PRELUDES

Sunday, November 9, 1981

The driver of the large tractor-trailer unit yawned. He'd risen early, and had picked-up the trailer from a factory in Mississauga. It was now several hours later. The sun was just rising, traffic was light, and he was looking forward to delivering his cargo. The manifest listed it as a prototype Amelior-8 manufactured by a company named Accelerated Nuclear Inc. He'd never heard of either, and had initially balked at the idea of transporting some kind of nuclear device, but had relented when it was explained to him that the device was neither a nuclear reactor, nor a nuclear weapon, but was simply a new device for treating cancers using electrons and X-rays. He'd heard of X-ray machines of course, but he didn't know what electrons and X-rays were, but at least the machine wasn't a bomb or a weapon. That and the bonus he'd been offered, "as an expression of the shipper's appreciation for his assistance in getting the device to the Toronto General Hospital for testing and evaluation."

He yawned again. Time for coffee, he thought. When the highway signs next displayed the food and fuel images, he took the off-ramp and parked at a large truck-stop. He didn't take any particular notice of the medium-grey van behind him that took the same off-ramp and parked a short distance away in the same parking lot. There was no particular reason why he should have noticed that the driver of the van got out at about the same time he did, and entered the coffee shop just behind him.

1

Intending to get his coffee in a to-go cup, his first stop was the bathroom. The bathroom was empty as he headed for one of the urinals, only dimly hearing the sounds of another person entering the bathroom. He'd just begun to relieve himself when he felt someone brush-up against him from behind, followed by an extremely sharp and intense pain radiating from one ear to somewhere inside his head. His body slumped almost immediately, as he lost control — and consciousness — and was only prevented from falling by the man behind him, who had placed an arm under each of his armpits.

The man from behind — the van's driver, in fact — dragged the truck driver to the one large toilet stall and arranged the body so that it was seated on the toilet and slumped against the near wall. Having stepped back to reassure himself that the body looked as normal as was possible in the circumstances, he searched for and removed the man's key ring. Then, he used damp paper towels to clean up the small amount of blood that had trickled from the truck driver's ear With all that accomplished, he left the stall and, with the help of a tool designed for the purpose, locked the door from the outside and left the bathroom.

Once out in the parking lot, the van driver waved to another tractor unit that had previously been following the van. As it started up, the van driver opened up the target tractor, disconnected and jacked up the trailer, then climbed into the cab and drove it to another spot in the lot. The driver of the second tractor unit swung over and backed up close to the unattached trailer, then got out to lower it onto the fifth-wheel plate, making sure that the king-pin engaged properly, then got out to connect the electrical and compressed-air lines. When all of this had been completed both the van and the tractor-trailer unit, with its stolen trailer, drove out of the parking lot and turned back the way they had come, heading northward toward Barrie.

After about an hour's drive they reached Barrie and proceeded to a truck stop with a large, drive-in truck wash of the self-serve, wand-wash type. It wasn't busy so early in the morning, so the driver was able to drive the entire unit right in. As the big door was closing, the truck driver exited and climbed up behind the cab, where an extendable ladder was attached. By the time he had freed the ladder from its attachments, he had been joined by the van driver who helped him extend the ladder and set it up beside the large trailer. The van driver had brought with him a duffel bag, from which he extracted the first of many cans of aerosol, quick-drying paint. Taking a couple of cans with him, the truck driver climbed the ladder and crawled up onto the roof, after which the van driver mounted the ladder but only to a point near the top of the trailer. Both men began painting the trailer.

As the van driver painted one side, he worked his way down the ladder, then moved the ladder over by a few feet, and repeated the process, something he did over and over again until he covered the entire side of the trailer. By this time the truck driver had finished painting the top, so he climbed down the ladder, after which both men began painting the other side, one working from the ladder on the upper portions while the other worked his way around the entire rest of the trailer painting as much as he could reach from the ground.

Within an hour, the entire trailer had been painted in a flat, medium-grey colour that completely hid both the colours and logos that it had formerly displayed. As a final touch, the van driver removed a licence plate from the duffel bag and replaced the trailer's original plate. When this was done, the two men placed the original licence plate and all of the empty spray cans into the duffel bag, which the van driver took back to the van. The truck driver then raised the truck-wash's large exit door and drove the truck out.

The van driver took one more walk around the tractor-trailer, inspecting it in the early morning sunlight, made a satisfied-sounding grunt. It was far from a professional-looking paint job, but once it had picked up some dirt and grime from the highway travel it would look like any other drab trailer. He gave the truck driver a thumbs-up signal.

Both vehicles then drove back onto the highway, heading toward Sudbury, after which they would take the Trans-Canada Highway, heading for Western Canada.

It was another hour before the dead body was discovered in the bathroom of the first truck-stop, 30 minutes before the police and ambulance arrived, and another two hours before anyone realized that the trailer had been stolen. By the time the police had been alerted and begun to search for the trailer, the thieves had reached Sudbury, nearly 450 km away. But it was worse than that because no one knew what

3

direction the trailer went, and no one knew that it had been repainted, nor that it had its licence plate switched.

***

The Daily News

Sunday, November 9, 1981

Miracle Cancer-Treatment Device Stolen from Accelerated Nuclear

Seven months later,
Sunday, June 6, 1982
Saskatoon, Saskatchewan

In terms of physical attributes, Harland Walker looked like the stereotypical, or even Hollywood conception of a senator hailing from the Southern United States. He had a solid build, was reasonably tall, and had a full head of snow-white hair, a white moustache, and a white, pointed, goatee beard. He spoke with a southern accent and he even walked with a cane, although he was perfectly capable of walking without it. Conveniently enough, he really was a U.S. Senator and he was shrewd enough to emphasize, rather than diminish, his resemblance to the stereotype.

The one somewhat jarring note, as he disembarked from the jetliner on which he'd arrived, was his clothing, which bore no resemblance whatsoever to the senatorial stereotype. This was because he was dressed in the khaki 'bush-attire' that he regarded as an appropriate outfit for someone heading for a fly-in fishing trip. The only exception was his trademark white Stetson hat. It wasn't his best hat to be sure. It was in fact his oldest and most heavily worn Stetson, but it meant that anyone glancing at him for the first time would immediately be put in mind of the classic southern-gentleman image.

When the Customs and Immigration official asked about his purpose in visiting Canada, he declared himself to be on a fly-in fishing trip to Lake Athabasca in northern Saskatchewan. He presented a brochure from a fly-in fishing camp known as Athabasca Outfitters, plus his booking receipt/travel itinerary but the official merely examined his passport, then returned it and wished him a good trip. The senator's itinerary showed that he would be connecting to a small plane to fly to Prince Albert, then to a plane to Uranium City, and then to a float plane that would take him to a fishing camp on Lake Athabasca. He further volunteered that he had no fishing gear with him as everything was to be supplied once he reached the camp.

Although unfamiliar with the name of this particular fishing camp, everything else aligned so perfectly with the stories of dozens of American fishers that patronized Saskatchewan's northern fishing camps that the official had no qualms whatsoever about welcoming the visitor to Canada and passing him through.

Accordingly, three plane trips later, the senator found himself landing on Lake Athabasca itself. When the float plane had taxied to an old-looking wharf and he had disembarked, he was met by a distinguished-looking man who identified himself as Dr. Ernst Wildersbach.

"Welcome, welcome," said the latter, shaking the senator's hand enthusiastically. "How was your trip? No trouble with Customs and Immigration I trust?"

"No trouble at all," replied the senator, "I'm just tired from all the travelling."

"Of course, of course," said the doctor. "If you're not too tired, we'll offer you a nice hot meal and then show you to your cottage. Tomorrow, we'll show you everything – explain everything – and then we can begin."

"I must admit that I am extremely curious about everything, but I agree that some food will be all that I can remain awake for."

"Fine, fine. I will lead you to the dining hall and then I will have one of my assistants show you to your cottage. Don't worry about your luggage, it will be waiting for you when you get there. I must apologize for not spending more time with you this evening, but I assure you that you will have my fullest attention in the morning."

"And the treatment?" the senator tried but failed to keep a slight note of desperation from his voice.

"Absolutely, absolutely. I will show you everything. We will take some X-rays, then I will explain everything, and then we will begin the treatment immediately after that. Tomorrow morning without fail." The doctor led the senator to a pickup truck, motioned for the senator to get in, and then he himself took up position in the driver's seat.

Feeling somewhat reassured, the senator got into the truck and settled into his seat. As they drove around the metal-clad warehouse-type building that stood in front of the dock, they almost immediately passed a towering structure that had been the site's most eye-catching feature when the float-plane had circled the site before landing on the lake.

"What is this place anyway?"

"Ah, yes. There's quite a story here. We're using a ghost town. All the structures you're going to see here are part of an abandoned uranium mining operation left over from the cold war[1]. It was built in the 1950s

to provide uranium for your own country's nuclear weapons program. The big tower is the headframe for the hoist that serviced the underground mine. If you look to your right, you will see what looks like a small lake."

"It looks artificial," said the senator, noting that it was oval in shape and appeared to be nearly a quarter mile long. His estimate was close; it was actually a thousand feet (300 m) long.

"That's very observant of you. They began with a large open-pit mine, then did the underground workings later. When everything was shut-down in the 1960s, they blasted to create a connection between the underground workings and the bottom of the open pit, then they blasted a channel between the pit and the lake, and voilá, the open-pit and underground workings were completely flooded up to the level of the big lake itself, which is what you see now.

"The buildings you can see to our left were warehouses and mine maintenance shops, and up ahead you can just see the mill where they processed the ore to produce yellowcake uranium concentrate. It was all very self-contained. Behind the mill there's a huge acid plant – they made their own sulphuric acid for the mill here – and there's a concrete plant too." The doctor turned left. "That building on our right was the powerhouse, but the generators were salvaged long ago so we have had to bring in our own diesel generators. Ah. Here we are. This is the original cookhouse. You can just see some of the large bunkhouses behind it."

"I thought you said I'd be staying in a cottage," said the senator, sounding surprised and possibly a bit grumpy.

"I did. I certainly did. The bunkhouses are all quite derelict now and I suspect that the upper floors may be quite unsafe. There is much more to the site than you've seen so far. They built an entire townsite here: a department store, community centre, hospital, school, and a nice little collection of small houses, some of which we have fixed up quite nicely. When I mentioned a cottage, I was referring to one of the fixed-up little houses. You will find it quite comfortable. Quite comfortable."

"Why was it shut down?" asked the senator, still thinking about what he had seen on their short drive.

"Mined out the entire orebody. They kept the mill running a little longer, to process the last of the mined ore. By the early 1960s, Canada, the U.K., and the U.S. all had more than the uranium they felt they needed, so the uranium price began to fall. By the mid-1960s the uranium market had crashed, causing most of the local mines to close. That meant they couldn't even process ore for other mines, so they shut down the mill here, and the entire community left, virtually overnight. At its peak, the town had about 850 people. By 1964 it was a ghost town. Later on, you can borrow one of our vehicles and drive around it as much as you like. It's all quite fascinating, really."

"How did you manage to take it all over?" asked the senator, still trying to get his mind around the doctor's story.

"I leased it from the provincial government, of course. It was just sitting here abandoned and in the middle of nowhere. The government had a loan program aimed at entrepreneurs and start-up businesses, so..."

"You borrowed the capital on the promise of new jobs and increased tourism and used the money to pay the same government for the lease," finished the Senator with a smile. This was something he could understand.

"Exactly, exactly."

"And do you actually run a fly-in fishing camp here?"

"As far as anyone knows, yes. We have fishing gear and boats, and some of our staff are knowledgeable enough to be able to take people out fishing. Our boats go out every day," he said with a wink, "although normally it's just our own people going out to fish and keep up appearances. But we do take our patients out as well, if they are interested. You will be welcome to go out yourself if you wish, in between treatments. The fishing is really quite good. Quite good."

"And no one knows anything about what you really do here?"

"No, no. Dear me, no," he said, then immediately contradicted himself, "The staff know, of course, and our agents and former patients know, otherwise our word-of-mouth business would very quickly become extinct."

"Just like the old uranium mine," observed the senator.

"Exactly, exactly. A very apt comparison," he chuckled.

"But why, doctor? Your agent explained the services you provide, and supplied patient references — which I checked out quite thoroughly — but he was quite vague about the need for secrecy. Kept insisting that it was the only way to keep the waiting lists short and provide rapid access to the treatments. But I'm not so easy to fool as all that. There's more to your story than exclusivity isn't there?" He gave the doctor a penetrating look from under his bushy white eyebrows.

"Well, you're right. Absolutely right. Yes indeed. The part our agent told you about is partly true, of course. Secrecy and premium prices enable us to maintain next to no waiting time for our treatments, which enables wealthy patients such as yourself to avoid the long waits that everyone else has to endure in America, Canada, and most other countries around the world for that matter." He gave the senator a shrewd look. "But there is another reason. Our state-of-the-art radiation machine is unlicensed, so we can hardly admit that we have it, much less that we are using it to treat cancers and save lives."

"Unlicensed! But... but..." the senator began to sputter.

"Now, now. Calm yourself, senator. There is no cause for concern. No cause for concern at all, I assure you. Our radiation treatment machine has been fully tested and is completely safe as long as it is being used by trained professionals, which is what we have here. And it's not experimental, dear me no. Our unit is what is called the production prototype, meaning that it is the same as the ones that will soon be rolling off assembly lines but this one was very carefully built by hand. To the exact same specifications as the future production ones will be, but carefully built by hand. Everything has been done excepting only that the regulatory approval process is very slow. I don't have to tell you how slowly the wheels of government machinery move." He looked the senator in the eye. "No. I can see that you do understand. The regulatory process takes years when anything nuclear is involved, and it takes even longer when new technologies are developed. But otherwise, all the testing and certifications are complete. I will even show you the documentation tomorrow. Please. No more question for now. Let us go inside and I will introduce you to the dining room staff. As I said earlier, I promise to be available to answer any and all of your questions tomorrow after breakfast. Then, we will only proceed if you feel completely satisfied."

"And if I don't?"

"Why, my good sir, if you do not feel completely satisfied then we will take no further steps. We can assist you with new travel arrangements and you may leave whenever you wish." He paused, for effect, then smiled. "You can even go fishing first, with one of our guides, if you *like."*

The two men walked into the dining hall. "This is our main dining room. You'll find a meal schedule in the house you've been assigned to. The house will have a fully functional kitchen stocked with a few necessities like coffee and snacks but, for anything substantial, everyone eats together here in the dining room. It's all very friendly and informal." Then, after introducing the senator to one of the dining hall staff, the doctor took his leave.

A good, hot meal left the senator somewhat mollified, and when he was later guided to one of the nearby houses, he was surprised to see that it was very comfortably appointed, which provided a confidence boost.

Early the next morning, Dr. Wildersbach met the senator as he was finishing his breakfast. "How are you feeling this morning, Senator? Ready for your first treatment?"

"I sure am. In fact, I'm feeling finer than a frog hair split four ways"

"Fine. Fine," said the doctor, struggling to understand the expression but pleased at the Senator's obvious enthusiasm. When you're ready, we'll walk over to the hospital and take some X-rays. Then we'll begin."

A short while later, the X-rays having been taken and developed, the doctor put one of the films up on the lighted viewing box that was mounted on the wall. "If you look right here," he pointed to a rather fuzzy spot on the upper back and slightly to one side of the spine, "that's the location from which your surgeon removed the cancerous tumor." The senator nodded. He'd been shown something like this before.

"Our job now," continued the doctor, "is to attack the little bits of growth that have been left behind. For that, we'll be using the Amelior-8, which is the very first of a new generation of machines that will be produced by Accelerated Nuclear Inc. once they receive regulatory approvals, as I mentioned to you last night." The senator nodded again.

"The machine is what is called a medical linear accelerator[2], and what it does is accelerate electrons to create high-energy beams that can destroy cancerous tumors with very little impact on the nearby tissue. In your case the main tumor was quite close to your spine, so we can treat it with just an electron beam. If it had been deeper inside your body, then we'd have had to convert the electrons into X-rays but there's no need for that in your case.

"What we're going to do is treat you once a day until we're sure that we've completely removed all of the cancerous cells."

"My own doctor said that this could be done in as little as four weeks," the senator said, hopefully.

"Well now, that's possible. Yes, certainly possible, but I can't promise you that. You have to understand that it might take a little longer, but I'm quite confident that it won't be more than six weeks."

The senator nodded. He'd been told this as well. *"When will you be able to begin?"*

"Right now, of course. Right now," said the doctor, nodding his head. *"Yes. Yes, just follow me and we'll go down the hall to our treatment room. This was the original mine hospital, you know,"* he explained, as they proceeded out and down the hallway. *"It had seven beds, a resident doctor, and four nursing staff, making it just the right size for us here. All we had to do was renovate some of the rooms and add the dedicated power generator that you probably heard running when we walked over here."*

As the doctor led the way through a new doorway, the senator could see that they were in a small control room where a young woman immediately stood up from a computer display to greet them.

"This is Lisa," introduced the doctor. *"She's the technician that will be operating the machine. Lisa, you have the prescription for the senator's treatment: electron beam treatment of 180 rads at 22 MeV."*

"Yes, doctor."

"Fine. Fine. Senator, I will leave you in Lisa's capable hands, and I will come back and check on you in a little while." So saying, the doctor took his leave.

"Come with me Senator," said Lisa, *"and we'll get everything set-up for you."* She led him into the treatment room and had him lie face-down on the treatment table. *"Comfortable? Fine. As you can see. I'm moving the table and rotating the gantry so that the treatment beam will be aimed exactly where we want it. There. Now I'm adjusting the treatment field size – that means the area that we want to be targeted by the electron beam... there. Now, I'm going to leave the treatment room and sit down at the computer console. You'll just be able to see where I am if you look through that little window in the wall. OK?"*

"Yes, fine."

"Great. Now then, when I get there, I will switch on the intercom so we can speak to each other." Lisa left the room, closed the door and settled-in at her computer terminal, from which position she could also control the intercom.

"Senator? Can you hear me?"

"Yes," came the Senator's surprised sounding voice. "In fact, I can hear you very clearly."

"Excellent. I will give you a running commentary on what I'm doing while you just lie there and relax and try not to move your body."

"I'll try." Came the reply.

"Fine. The machine and computer are on, and I am just typing in your name and the machine settings: that means the gantry rotation, field sizing, and a few other mechanical details. The computer will check to make sure that the data I enter matches the settings I just made manually when I was in there with you. It will only allow me to proceed if they match perfectly. That's for your safety, you see."

The Senator could actually hear the clicking sounds as she pushed the keys on the keyboard. Lisa, meanwhile was reading the lines as they came up on her display:

```
PATIENT NAME: WALKER, HARLAND
DATE: 82-JUN-07 TIME: 09:30
OPR ID: LISA


TREATMENT MODE: X ENERGY        BEAM ENERGY (MeV):22


                            ACTUAL  PRESCRIBED
GANTRY ROTATION (DEG):         0.0         0.0      OK
COLLIMATOR ROTATION (DEG):   359.2         359      OK
COLLIMATOR X (CM):            14.2        14.0      OK
COLLIMATOR Y (CM):            27.1        27.0      OK
WEDGE NUMBER:                    1           1      OK
ACCESSORY NUMBER:                0           0      OK
```

"OK. Everything is looking good... Oops. I made I typing error. Just a moment." Lisa had noticed that she'd accidentally typed 'x' (for X-ray) when she had intended to type 'e' (for electron) mode. This was because most of the treatments involved X-rays, and she had gotten used

to typing this. On the other hand, she'd been operating the machine for some time and was used to quickly making changes using the system's editing features. Using the 'cursor-up' key, she edited the treatment mode entry from 'x' to 'e'.

```
TREATMENT MODE: ELECTRON      BEAM ENERGY (MeV):22
```

Checking to make sure that the other parameters she had entered were still correct, she hit the return key several times to pass through them while leaving their values unchanged. The next line on the display read:

```
SYSTEM: BEAM READY      OP. MODE: TREAT      AUTO
```

"OK. I've fixed the error and rechecked everything else." Lisa then hit the one-key command B, for beam on, to begin the treatment.

```
TREATMENT MODE: E ENERGY      BEAM ENERGY (MeV):22

                          ACTUAL PRESCRIBED
UNIT RATE/Minute:            0       200
MONITOR UNITS:               8       200
TIME (MIN):               0.04      1.0
```

The machine switched on, but only for a few seconds, after which the display showed 8 monitor units delivered, which was a severe underdose considering she had set the machine to deliver 200 monitor units. She had become quite used to the machine's eccentricities, however, which caused it to halt or pause from time to time without warning. In this case, she interpreted the machine's underdosing as just another unexpected pause and did what she always did in such cases: tap the P key to resume treatment. The machine promptly shut down with messages reporting that treatment had been paused and a MALFUNCTION 66 error code.

TREAT: TREAT PAUSE   REASON: MALFUNCTION   66

At the same time, she heard a scream from inside the treatment room. Getting up and rushing into the room, she found the Senator scrambling off of the table and attempting to stand up.

"Are you all right? Let me help you," she said as she grabbed one of his arms and steered him to a nearby chair.

"What in God's name was that?" he gasped. "There was a thump and what felt like a huge electric shock to my back, and it felt hot, very hot."

"Just sit right here and I will go get the doctor. It will only be a moment." Forcing herself to appear calm and professional, she walked out of the room and turned the corner. Then, out of sight of the Senator, she ran to the outer hallway and along it looking for Dr. Wildersbach.

The machine, meanwhile, sat quietly continuing to display the malfunction message. A typed sheet taped to the side of the computer monitor held a listing of malfunction error codes. For MALFUNCTION 66 it read "dose input error," which the machine's operating manual explained meant that the dose delivered had been either too high or too low. Unbeknown to either Lisa or Dr. Wildersbach, the prototype machine had some programming bugs, one of which was that some of the machine settings — such as the orientation of the bending and focusing magnets - changed fairly slowly, whereas the prescription data could be edited very quickly — more quickly in fact, than the machine was programmed to check for such changes. This sometimes led to mismatches between the computer values being displayed and the machine settings actually in place. In some cases, this led to inadvertent but severe overdosing[3].

When Lisa returned to the treatment room with Dr. Wildersbach, he immediately examined the senator and discovered a skin burn spanning the area treated. They moved him to a bed in the one hospital ward that was still being maintained, all the while assuring the senator that he had simply had a bad reaction to the treatment, and that it would clear in time.

"Does this mean you won't be able to continue the treatments?" the senator asked.

"No, we should be able to do another one tomorrow, as scheduled. You just rest quietly here for now and I will come and have another look at you later this afternoon."

When Dr. Wildersbach examined him that afternoon, however, the 'burn' looked much worse. He didn't admit this to the senator, however, and instead told him that they would like to keep him overnight in the hospital, but that they would resume treatments the next day, as planned. Then, he went to run some diagnostics on the machine itself.

"What do you think doctor?" asked Lisa, after he had checked all of the machine settings.

"The damn thing has done it again. It delivered a massive dose instead of the one I prescribed."

"But, I assure you, I made sure everything on the display was reading exactly as it should before pressing the 'P' key to proceed."

"I know. I know. And nineteen times out of twenty, the machine delivers exactly the dose that has been selected, but in one time out of twenty it delivers something different: either too much or too little radiation. Someday, Accelerated Nuclear is going to discover that either there is a bug in the computer software, or else an intermittent electrical fault in the linear accelerator, and fix it. But, for now, this machine is all we have to work with."

"Do you think the senator is going to die like the others?"

"I don't know yet, Lisa, but it's certainly possible. Yes, certainly possible. We may have to console ourselves with the thought that we are able to save the lives of most of our patients, but not all of them."

In fact, the senator had indeed received a massive overdose, concentrated in the treatment location but extending to his spine.

Over the weeks following the accident, they continued with his treatments knowing that they would probably only make matters worse. As a result, the senator began to experience pain in his back, then in his shoulders, and eventually in his extremities. Within four weeks, the senator had extreme difficulty moving his limbs and became unable to walk. The doctor concluded, correctly, that the senator had developed radiation myelopathy of the cervical spine, but did not admit this to anyone, much less the patient, who died in week four.

Although they had not lost a large number of patients due to treatment malfunctions, they had developed a procedure for dealing with them. The doctor had two specific, highly-trusted orderlies for such work, whom he called in to remove the body. The first stages of this removal were conducted with the utmost dignity and decorum, with the body encased in a standard body-bag, placed on a gurney, and covered with a clean sheet. The orderlies then took it from the building and drove it to a location beside the flooded mine pit, but on the far side and well away from the normally travelled roads. There they placed the body bag into a rowboat that was moored there.

Later that night, the two orderlies returned to the boat bringing with them a heavy chain from one of the machine shops. Then, they rowed out to the centre of the flooded pit, wrapped and secured the chain around the body bag, then carefully eased it over the side and into the water. The body bag went in without a sound and immediately sank the 110 m (360 ft.) to the bottom. In Dr. Wildersbach's judgement, the odds of anyone going SCUBA-diving in a pit filled with radioactive water, much less to a depth of 110 m, were low indeed.

All patients admitted for treatment were sworn to the utmost secrecy, but of course some violated this by, for example, telling a spouse where they were going. This is what had happened in the senator's case. When, therefore, enquiries were made about the 'senatorial fishing-guest' who had gone missing, the staff explained that the Senator had indeed come for a most relaxing fishing expedition, had declared himself to have had a very good time, and had been flown by seaplane to Uranium City, and from there by a chartered plane to the Prince Albert airport, then by commercial aircraft to Saskatoon, and finally connecting to a U.S.-bound flight.

What no one admitted to, was that it had been a member of the staff, dressed in the senator's clothes, made-up to resemble the senator in appearance, and carrying the senator's passport and other documents, that had made the flights — even to the extent of boarding the first flight cross-border in to the U.S., in this case to Denver. Once in Denver, the *staff member, who had a change of clothing in his carry-on bag, changed his appearance back to normal, discarded the senators clothing and documents, and boarded a return flight to Canada under his own name.*

When a worried senator's wife hired a private detective to attempt to locate her husband, he found — as he was intended to - that the trail went cold in Denver.

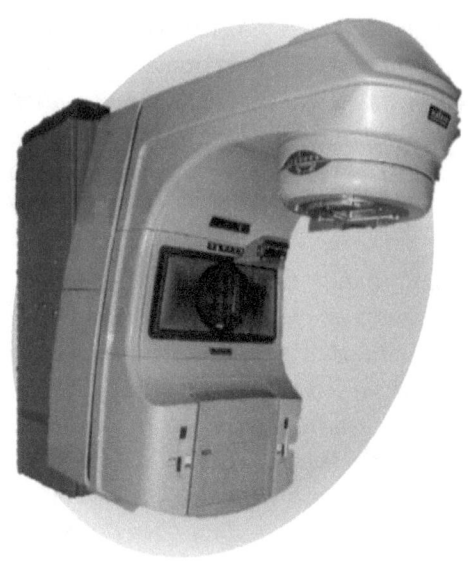

Sunday, July 24, 1982
Saskatoon, Saskatchewan

One of the first arrivals at the airport this Sunday morning was a Boeing 737 in the livery of one of America's largest airlines. The big jet touched down without incident and taxied to the terminal building. Among the passengers that disembarked and made their way to Canada Customs and Immigration was a man with brown hair and eyes; with average looks; was of average height and build; and he looked - ordinary. So ordinary, in fact, that if you passed him in the street nothing about his appearance would catch your attention. This was one of his skills: looking so unremarkable as to be virtually invisible in a crowd. He had many other skills as well.

His American passport identified him as Robert Johnson. That wasn't his real name, but it was a common enough name. The names Robert and Johnson were the second most common first and surnames, respectively, in the United States. Not the absolute most common, however, that would be James Smith, but even that could have attracted the attention of an unusually alert customs and immigration official, and Robert Johnson did not want to attract anyone's attention just yet.

When the official asked about his purpose in visiting Canada, he declared himself to be on a fly-in fishing trip to Lake Athabasca in northern Saskatchewan and offered to present a booking receipt/travel itinerary.

He certainly looked the part. Although Robert Johnson's trip to Canada resembled that embarked upon by Senator Harland Walker a month and a half earlier, there were some notable differences. Although his clothing was the kind of wilderness-adventure clothing common to visiting American tourists heading for a northern hunting- or fishing-camp adventure, the tourists' clothing was generally brand-new, or at least in excellent condition. Johnson's clothing, on the other hand, had clearly seen better days as it showed every sign of hard use – faded, stained, patched, frayed in places, and almost threadbare. Almost, threadbare, that is. A very careful examination would have shown that it was still as strong and functional as it had been when purchased new. Similar descriptions could be applied to his luggage, which looked equally travelled and worn: a backpack and duffel bag – both in camouflage pattern – and a long cylindrical case with a shoulder strap, of the kind used to carry fishing rods. Everything about him seemed so commonplace that, having looked him over, the official simply stamped and returned his passport without even hesitating, then wished him a good trip.

Johnson, and several other similarly clothed and equipped passengers from the same incoming flight, had a short wait then boarded a twin-engine turboprop plane to fly to Prince Albert. From there, the other passengers transferred to different planes, presumably on their way to some of the many fly-in fishing camps that are distributed around Saskatchewan's north which, contrary to the Saskatchewan stereotype of endlessly flat prairie, almost completely comprises lakes and forests. Johnson himself was scheduled to fly directly to the former Gunnar uranium mine site on a dedicated charter aircraft, rather than connecting through Uranium City, but he had some time before the flight.

Having collected his baggage, he carried it with him into the terminal's one 'Family Washroom.' After locking the door, he changed clothes and also changed the appearance of his baggage, in the latter case by the simple expedient of unzipping the close-fitting covers that encased his backpack and duffel bag. With their covers off, the backpack and duffel bag were revealed to be a medium-brown khaki colour, and both of them in excellent condition. Even the fishing-rod case had a zippered cover removed, revealing the standard black plastic of a traditional, shoulder-slung map case. Tucking the zippered covers into the duffel bag, he re-entered the terminal proper. Anyone chancing to look at the man exiting from the family washroom would have seen a man in the summer uniform of a government conservation officer, complete with crested, dark-blue baseball cap, and wearing sunglasses.

In the unlikely event that he encountered a real such conservation officer in the brief time he'd be spending in the air terminal, he had a cover story involving being sent out to conduct a series of surprise fisheries and wildlife compliance checks (including selected fly-in fishing camps) plus environmental inspections related to such things as shoreline alteration, unlawful dumping, and so on. He would then express extreme surprise that the local conservation officer had not been notified in advance, offer his apologies and suggest that the real officer 'take it up' with the head office in Regina. That would, of course, take some time and the fly-in fishing camp at Gunnar had no telephone service.

As it turned out, no one questioned his assumed identity and his charter float plane eventually arrived to pick him up and fly him directly to the Gunnar site. It was late afternoon when they crossed Lake Athabasca, landed, and taxied to the Gunnar dock. While the pilot was busy tying up the plane, they were met by a man dressed like a local and who identified himself as Ben Delorme one of the camp's fishing guides. But, quickly assessing his manner and the way he carried himself, Johnson figured him to be more like a guard than a guide. He'd expected something like this and launched into his cover story.

Delorme asked them to wait and stepped away in order to be able to speak to someone on a handheld radio.

VHF radio, Johnson thought to himself. He was able to overhear a few of the words, enough to verify that Delorme was relating his story to someone with more authority. It wasn't long before Delorme came back.

"Spoke to the owner. He's just up near the town and will come right down. It will only be a few minutes."

"Fine," replied Johnson, stepping over to select a sturdy-looking wooden crate to sit on, from which position he took out a cigarette package and waved it towards Delorme in offering. Delorme, for his part, seemed surprised but didn't hesitate to approach and take one. Having lit cigarettes for each of them, Johnson leaned back and relaxed, noting as he did that Delorme stepped back to smoke his. Johnson nodded approvingly, Delorme had placed himself between the dock, where Johnson was relaxing, and the rest of the site – just like a guard would.

Ten minutes later a pickup truck rounded the corner of the warehouse and approached the men. An older man got out of the truck and walked over.

"I understand you're here for some kind of surprise inspection. Have we done something wrong? My name is Dr. Ernst Wildersbach, by the way." He put a hand out to shake. "Retired doctor that is, I'm the owner of Athabasca Outfitters. We have a lease on the old Gunnar mine-site, as I'm sure you know."

"Yes, I do, and no you haven't done anything wrong. At least, nothing I'm aware of. It's the Ministry's policy to conduct a certain number of surprise fisheries and wildlife compliance checks every season. We probably do about a third of them each year, so each operation only gets checked once every three years or so. That way there's a regular

pattern, and paper-trail, of inspections without having to burden each operator every year with the inconvenience of having us trapse around sticking our noses into everything every year. Of course," he added deprecatingly, *"the rare operation that flaunts the regulations gets checked much more regularly, but we don't want to interfere with the good operators which, to be fair, represent the vast majority."*

"Very reasonable. In fact, a surprisingly reasonable attitude for a government regulator to take. No offense, mind you."

"None taken. Call it a balancing act. The government wants operators like you to run your businesses here, the tourism business is an important part of the economy, but we have a job to do as well."

"Fine, fine. But what's happened to Mike, our regular conservation officer?"

"Nothing, as far as I know." Johnson affected surprise. *"The Ministry is experimenting with having dedicated officers do these inspections. In fact, these inspections are the only thing I'll be doing during the tourist season this year. I started on the May long weekend, and I'll be doing them until just after the Labour Day Weekend in the fall – all over the province. I guess someone higher up thinks that the local officers are at risk of becoming too complacent about their assigned areas, or something like that. Anyway, your regular guy will do spot checks, but my job is to look the whole operation over in a single sweep. In this case, it's a bigger job than usual because you've leased the entire site even though you're probably only using pieces of it."*

The doctor nodded. *"That's right. We greet our customers here, feed them in the dining hall, house them in some of the smaller houses, and run the boats out of that little marina that's near where the curling rink and school used to operate. We also use this warehouse for storage and the old machine shops for repairing our boats and vehicles."*

"Makes sense to me," said Johnson, *"but I'm afraid I have to look over the whole operation, including the head-frame, mill, acid plant, community housing and buildings, tailings areas, and even the shoreline."*

"That will take some time," said the doctor.

"Actually, it won't be too bad. Most places I just need to peek into and move on, and the parts that you are actually using won't need much more than quick glance. This is the first time I've visited this particular site, but I have the original Gunnar Mines maps and descriptions from

1957 to guide me."

"You're certainly welcome, but I'd like to have one of my staff act as your guide. I'm sure you can find your way, but some of these buildings are on the verge of collapse and it would be unfortunate and embarrassing for both our company and your department if you got injured while you were here. Besides, my man can chauffeur you around wherever you need to go, and he'll have a portable radio with him so he'll be able to call for help if you should find you need anything. We're not full up with customers right now, so we can spare someone without interfering with business."

"That's very good of you," said Johnson, *who'd expected nothing less.* Now for the tricky part, *he thought. He made a show of looking at his watch.* "I wonder…" *he said hesitantly.* "I was supposed to arrive here this morning and be finished by about now, but I had some unexpected delays. I can get the plane to fly me to Uranium City and find a place to stay overnight, unless…"

"Nonsense. There's no need for that at all. We can put you and your pilot up for the night, and then you can start your inspection first thing in the morning."

"Well, if you're sure…"

"Certainly, certainly. Always ready to cooperate with the government. You'll find the food here is excellent, especially if you enjoy fresh fish." He chuckled. *"We have a nice little two-bedroom house I can put at your disposal, if you and your pilot don't mind sharing?"*

"I'll talk to him, but I'm sure he'll agree. I'll offer to pay him double, and I think the thought of the extra money will make the decision for him."

"Fine. Fine. Talk to your pilot then bring your gear up to the truck and I'll drive you to the houses. Ben here will give you a hand." He looked meaningfully at Delorme who took his cue and began sauntering down to where the plane was tied up.

With their bags loaded into the truck, Johnson and his pilot climbed in with the doctor, who drove them to one of the houses that was within easy walking distance of the dining hall. Along the way he gave them the same description of the mine-site and its history that he gave all visitors to the site. In this case, however, he also drove by a small cove, pointing out that the mining company had constructed a small dock and barged in sand to make a beach for the staff to enjoy and launch small boats from. He explained that it provided some shelter from the big lake and that the pilot was welcome to move his aircraft there if he wanted. The pilot said he'd like to take a closer look at it before deciding, and Johnson offered to walk down with him after they'd settled their baggage in the house.

By this time, it was shortly before dinner would be served so the doctor suggested they take their look and then head for the dining hall.

"I may not be able to join you for dinner," he cautioned. "But I will certainly meet you after breakfast and make sure that you have anything you might need for your inspection." With that, he took his leave. As the two men carried their luggage in to the house, Johnson noted without surprise that Delorme, who had followed them in a separate truck, was parked not far away.

After a few minutes, the two men walked the 150 m (500 ft.) from their house to the marina so the pilot could look it over. There were a couple of beach chairs on the sand beach, several canoes stacked over to one side, and two small motorboats tied up at the dock. Over to one side of the small bay was another float plane, which was moored to a buoy and also secured by two ropes to trees on the shore. There was a second, unused, buoy not far away.

"What do you think?" Johnson asked the pilot.

He shrugged. "The weather forecast for tonight and tomorrow was clear, but the weather can change quickly on a lake this big. I think I'd feel safer moving the plane over here and using a three-point mooring arrangement like they've done with the one here."

"Take a look over my shoulder. Do you see a truck parked up the way behind us?"

The pilot looked up, then gave an exclamation of surprise. "Yes. Keeping an eye on us, I suppose?"

"Hmmm. Not very trusting, are they? See if you can get him to drive you back to the other dock so you can get the plane. If he's reluctant, make up some story about a forecasted storm brewing just out of sight and that you want to get the plane over here as soon as possible. He'll call in for instructions on his radio. See if you can overhear the conversation, will you? Meanwhile, I'll see if I can get one of these boats started so I can help you tie-up to the buoy and bring you back here. Do *you have ropes in the plane."*

"For tying up to the shore you mean? Sure. I've got ropes and cargo straps. We'll be able to jury-rig something." The pilot walked up the hill from the marina and spoke to Delorme. There was a delay, after which the pilot walked around the truck and got in. The truck drove away.

Dragging one of the chairs up from the beach, Johnson placed it on the dock in a position from which he could look out over the lake, but easily glance back up the hill to the road. Settling himself in, he lit another cigarette and made a show of looking out over the lake. Within a few minutes, he heard the sound of a truck approaching and then shut off. Being careful to only turn his head very slightly he was just able to discern that another pickup truck had parked such that the driver could keep an eye on him.

Oh no, my friends, you don't catch me out as easily as all that, *he thought to himself. He contentedly tipped his baseball cap down lower on his face and dropped his chin down towards his chest as if having a snooze while he waited for the plane to arrive.*

Later that evening, having secured the float-plane and having enjoyed a good meal in the dining room, the two men had walked back to their house for the night, followed at a discreet distance by one of the company's pickup trucks.

"They're not very good at this, are they?" asked the pilot, who knew Johnson was up to something, but not what.

"No. I've been watching them, and they seem like hired muscle that mostly do odd jobs around here. They're probably tough enough, and maybe even good in a fight, but they're not professionals."

"And you are?"

Johnson smiled grimly. "That's the kind of question you're being paid not to ask," he reproved.

"Sorry. What's next then?"

"Next, we wait for twilight." The two men entered the house and turned on all the lights. After an hour or two, they switched all the lights off.

"I'm going to watch for a while," Johnson said to the pilot. "Don't be surprised if I disappear for an hour or two. If anything happens to me just remember: you know nothing. You were simply hired to fly me here,

wait around, and then fly me out. Nothing more. In the worst case, they'll make up some story about me or invent some kind of excuse to get you to fly out of here: take it, and when you get back to civilization, phone the number I gave you. It's toll free. When someone answers, tell them you have a message from Sparrow. The message is: 'Hawk,' repeat that back to me." The pilot did so, twice. "That's it. Try to get some sleep. With luck, I'll see you in the morning."

For the next hour, Johnson prowled from room to room, pausing to the side of each window and silently watching for a while before moving on to the next. Within the first half hour, he had identified two watchers by the occasional lighting of their cigarettes. There was one watching the front, and another watching the back. Not bad, but not very original, thought Johnson, who went to change into dark grey shirt and pants, and then applied black camouflage face-paint and put on a black wool toque. From his duffel bag, he withdrew two sheathed knives, one of which he attached to his left forearm, under his shirt sleeve, and the other to his right calf, under his pant leg. The knives were identical, double-bladed throwing knives, the kind that are exceptionally dangerous in the hands of a trained professional. Johnson was a trained professional.

Checking the luminous hands on his watch showed that it was close to midnight. Twilight, he thought, and went to a side window that he'd previously opened. Moving carefully, he silently slipped out the window and lowered himself to the ground where he crouched, listening. Hearing nothing unusual, he crept silently towards the trees and melted into the forest.

Johnson knew that at such a high northern latitude, he would have only two hours of semi-darkness before it began to get brighter again. That meant he had to budget his time. There were several roads with similar houses on them, all accessible from the forest. Most of these he passed by with only the glance that was needed to verify that they were still in a state of abandonment and disrepair. Only a few, all of them close to the one he and the pilot shared, had been fixed up for guests but quick glances through the windows with the aid of a shielded penlight showed them to be currently unoccupied. Except... he had begun to turn away from the last window on the last house, when something made him turn back for a second look. It was a bedroom, and the bed had been made-up, but it looked like there was something pushed back under the *bed. Whatever it was, it wasn't visible unless someone deliberately looked under the bad, or viewed it from a shallow angle, as he was doing.*

Johnson crept around to the back of the house and tested the door. It was unlocked. Once again, he stopped and listened carefully for a few moments, as indeed he had been doing regularly on this excursion. Hearing nothing concerning, he opened the door and crept quietly to the indicated bedroom, reached under the bed, and withdrew a small, brown, well-worn leather briefcase of the kind that was then popular with civil servants and politicians. Opening the single clasp released the strap that held closed the expanding top, he opened the case. It contained a bottle of bourbon whiskey, several paperback novels, a notebook and pen, and a travel folio. Opening the folio, he used his penlight so he could scan the documents. They were the fishing-camp booking and travel documents, and business cards, of one Harland Walker.

Careless of someone, *thought Johnson, as he replaced everything in the case and put it back where he had found it. Then he got up, stretched, and noiselessly made his way out of the house and melted back into the forest. Checking his watch, he noted that he had time for one more stop. He decided on the hospital, which was only about 200 m (650 ft.) away. Pausing to get his bearings — he had previously memorized the mining company's maps and surface plans showing the locations of all of the significant structures on the site — he headed for the hospital, following game trails to the extent possible. Soon, he came upon the west side of the hospital, but crept around to the back.*

Sensing that there was no one around, he crept along each wall, pausing only long enough to shine his penlight into each window. The hospital was clearly in use, but nothing appeared to be out of the ordinary. If there's anything interesting, it will be on the inside or else on the second floor, *he thought, debating whether to attempt to enter the building or not. He checked his watch. There was just enough time left for a quick reconnoitre.*

Concerned that this might be the one building for which the doors and windows were alarmed, he looked higher up. On the outside of the building, there was an old-style steel fire escape from the second floor — the kind that had a section of the ladder suspended by springs so that it was well above the ground. From around his waist, he unwound a length of woven rope that was quite thin but extremely strong. He next searched around for an oblong-shaped rock. Finding one, he tied it to one end of the rope then experimented with tossing it up and toward the lower rungs of the suspended ladder. His aim being quite good, it only took three tries before the launched rock flew between two of the rungs, struck the side of the building and then fell to the ground. After untying the rock, he took both lengths of rope in both hands and tied them together so that the rope formed a loop that ended about two feet off the ground. Holding onto the ropes, he placed one foot into the bottom of the loop then slowly stepped up so that it carried his entire weight. With a scraping sound, the ladder came down two feet. As it did so, he extended his arms fully upward, grasped the ropes, and pulled down bringing the ladder all the way down. Then, having retrieved the rope and wrapped it around his waist, and having stood quietly for a few minutes to listen, he began to climb.

When he reached the top of the fire escape, he used one of his knives to open the simple latch on the window, slid the window open, and crawled in. It was dark inside, but he could tell that he was in a dormitory room of some kind. Using his pencil flashlight again, he confirmed his first impression: that it was not in use and had not been for many years. Carefully stepping around the debris that was scattered on the floor, he did a quick survey of the other rooms, discovering the entire floor to be a dormitory, with bunkrooms, washrooms, a laundry room, and a simple kitchen. His briefing hadn't included enough detail for him to know that this was where the nurses and other single women had been accommodated during the mine and mill's operating years.

There was a centrally-located staircase, which he descended. Finding himself in a hallway that appeared to run the entire length of the building, he surveyed this as well, locating the examination and treatment rooms, a seven-bed patients' ward, several offices, and what he took to be the doors to supply rooms. The first one he checked was, in fact a combination supply room and dispensary, while the other opened onto a small room containing a small desk bearing a computer and monitor, and another door bearing a radiation safety sign, and above which was mounted indicator light. Nodding to himself, he went in and opened the inner door. This latter room had no exterior windows and was pitch dark. His pencil flashlight revealed a large stand bearing a padded surface that was obviously meant for a patient to lie on. The stand was fitted with several mechanical levers and gears, which he took to be the means of moving the patient-bearing top up or down and left or right. To the left of the table was a tall, imposing machine that stood at a slight angle from the vertical. It was obviously some kind of radiation treatment machine that could rotate in a circular arc above a patient's body. Johnson nodded to himself, he had expected something like this, but they'd had to make sure.

Switching his flashlight off, he glanced at the luminous hands of his watch. Time to be leaving. This time he simply walked to the back door, carefully scanned all around the door's perimeter to check for alarm switches and, finding none, he unlocked and opened the door, then stepped out.

"Find anything interesting? asked a male voice as a blinding white light stabbed into his darkness-accustomed eyes. As he instinctively threw a hand up to shield his eyes while he tried to locate the source of the voice. he sensed - more than heard - something come close behind him. He was very quick to turn around, but whomever was behind him was faster. He felt, and even heard, something hard hit him at the base of the skull, and he was just beginning to feel the wave of pain when he collapsed, unconscious to the ground.

***

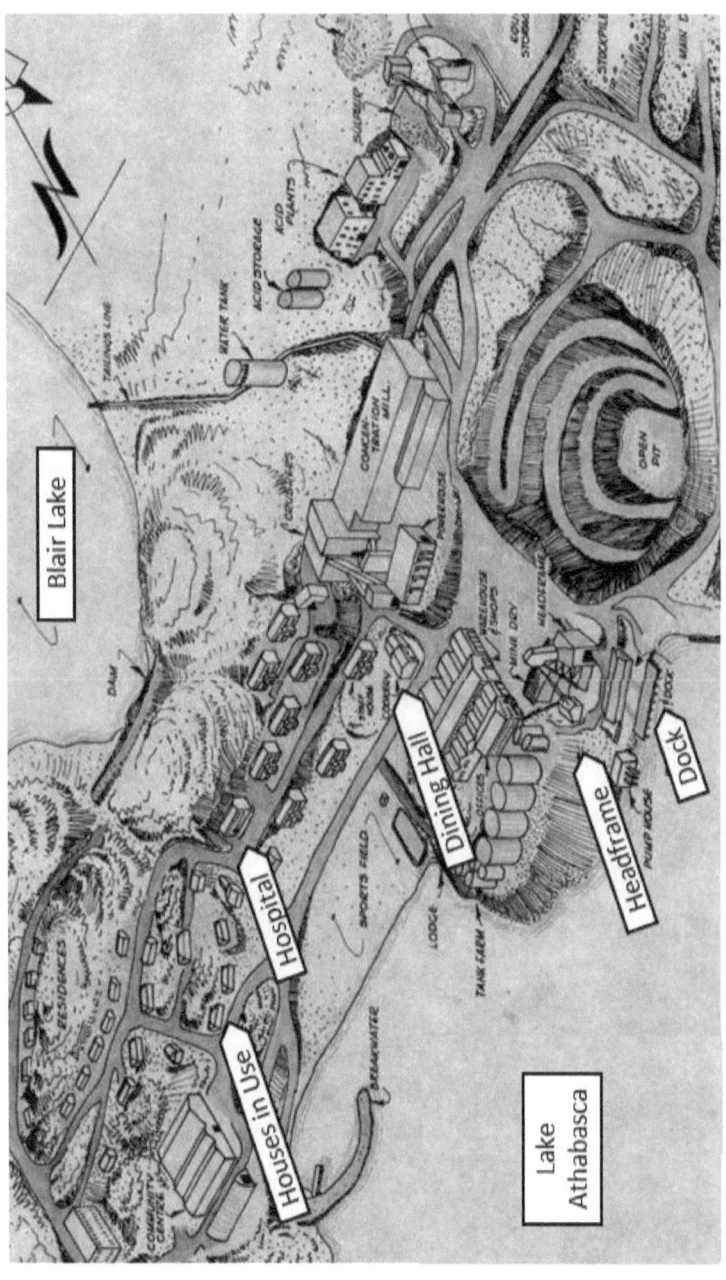

Laurie Schramm

2 A NEW ASSIGNMENT

Wednesday, July 28, 1982
RCMP Headquarters Building
Ottawa, ON

"He'll see you now," said the inspector who served as Executive Officer to Deputy Commissioner George MacLeod, the head of the RCMP's Security Service.

We must look like an unusual trio I thought as we rose from our chairs. My name is Alexandra Houston and, at the time, I was a Sergeant in the Security Service. Next to me was Silver, a large Alaskan Malamute; my long-time Police Service Dog partner and friend. Next to Silver was Major Donald Harrison, who served in military intelligence in the Canadian Forces and who was also my husband. It still seemed strange to think of him as my husband as we'd only been married for three months. After the wedding and honeymoon, Don had been assigned to a temporary position at National Defense Headquarters in Ottawa, which was giving us some time to decide how to handle our two-career marriage without having to live apart. We appreciatively suspected that Don's convenient assignment was the result of some kind of back-room deal between Deputy Commissioner MacLeod and Rear-Admiral White, the head of military intelligence. We were very grateful for that, but we'd thus far made no progress on how to reconcile our careers. On this particular day, we'd been summoned to the Deputy Commissioner's office and I couldn't help wondering whether fate was about to take a hand.

As the inspector stood aside, we made our way into the office of the man that had persuaded me to join the force in the first place, and who I sometimes referred to as 'Uncle George,' although never to his face. After taking a few steps inside, we stood to attention – even Silver – and in the momentary silence I noticed that, seated at his meeting table, Uncle George was accompanied by Admiral White and Staff Sergeant Avery Blunt, my immediate superior.

Uncle George told us to relax and, with a wave, indicated we should join them at the meeting table. "We all know each other too well for formalities," he said, as Don and I took our seats and Silver found a place to lie down nearby, "so let's get right to it." He nodded meaningfully at the admiral, who took over.

"We have an unusual situation, or, more correctly the CIA has a situation, and the Americans have asked for our help."

"That's odd, isn't it Sir?" asked Don, "They've always preferred to go their own way and keep their own counsel."

"They have gained that reputation, yes, but as I said the situation is unusual. Let me try to summarize what we think we know." He leaned forward over the edge of the table. "Several days ago, a private pilot made a phone call from the Fort McMurray Airport to a highly confidential number at Langley[4]. He said that he was relaying a message from Sparrow, and the message was 'Hawk.' That was the whole thing, a message from Sparrow comprising the single word 'Hawk.'"

"Sounds like secret-agent stuff from an old movie," I commented.

"So it does, but it set off alarm bells in the CIA. Apparently, they'd sent an undercover operative to snoop around one of the old, abandoned, Cold War uranium mine sites on the north shore of Lake Athabasca."

"Do you know which one?" I asked, suddenly more interested.

"We thought that would interest you. Yes. It was the old Gunnar mine," put in Uncle George.

"A fairly isolated mine and mill site. It was so remote they even had their own small townsite. I visited it once years ago, when I was stationed in the area."

"You will naturally be wondering what sparked the CIA's interest," resumed the admiral. "Back in June, a U.S. Senator flew up there, ostensibly for a fly-in-fishing vacation with an operator called Athabasca Outfitters, which has leased the site from the provincial government. There used to be a commercial fishing co-operative using part of the site but it closed last year. Apparently, the provincial government was more than willing to have another company have a try at building-up some local business in the area. In any case, the senator never returned home and, after a few days beyond his expected return, his wife hired a private detective to attempt to locate her husband. He discovered that the senator began his trip home but disappeared after landing in Denver.

"As you can imagine, that didn't do much to alleviate the senator's wife's concerns, so she called the FBI." The admiral paused to allow for the obvious questions, but Don and I remained silent so he could tell the story in his own way. With a nod, he continued.

"Right. The FBI took her call seriously and did some investigating. When they checked the Denver airport's security tapes, they showed the senator's wife some images of the man that presented the senator's passport to a U.S. Customs and Immigration officer. The wife insists that, although there's a superficial resemblance, the man in the photo is definitely not her husband. As they investigated further, the FBI learned that the fly-in-fishing operation is only a cover, and that the real reason the senator went there was for secret cancer treatments that would enable him to avoid the usual long waiting lists back home. Apparently, the availability of these cancer treatments is strictly word-of-mouth, but the FBI found a friend of the senator's that had gone for such treatments himself, and who had recommended them to the senator. It was only because of the senator's disappearance that this friend opened up to the FBI at all, since he'd apparently signed some kind of nondisclosure agreement that had stiff penalties for any violation of its terms.

"Obviously, something about this business is illegal or there'd be no need for such secrecy, or the remote location, or the fishing-camp ruse. The physicians might be unlicensed, or the treatments might be unusually risky and unlicensed, or something else, we don't know. But. Some people must think they work or there would be no word-of-mouth referrals and not many people would pay the outrageous fees being charged…. You with me so far?"

Don and I nodded.

"Once the FBI learned what I just told you someone, somewhere, decided that the CIA should send an undercover operative in to investigate." The admiral held up a hand to stave off the obvious question. "As you already pointed out, such an act is odd. The CIA routinely have operatives here in Canada, working in cooperation with our own intelligence personnel, but it's rare for them to send one in undercover, and without telling us. Of course, there's no way for us to know for sure how often, but we think it's pretty rare. They're our allies after all. It's not actually illegal, as long as they don't start breaking our laws, but any such clandestine operation of theirs on our soil could cause a major diplomatic embarrassment, so they wouldn't do it lightly."

"So why would they take the risk?" put in Uncle George, rhetorically. "I asked the FBI that directly. It turns out that Senator Harland Walker serves on the U.S. Senate Select Committee on Intelligence, which has oversight on the CIA, and which makes him important enough for them to want to find him quickly and quietly, if possible."

Wow! I thought. "You think they're worried that he defected to the Soviets?" I asked.

"That, or that the Soviets kidnapped him and are trying to extract intelligence from him."

"So, they sent someone in to follow the senator's trail," said Don.

The admiral nodded. "He flew the same route for most of the way, then chartered a float plane to get him to the Gunnar site. We don't know how he got access to the site, but he'd instructed the pilot that if he disappeared to phone a certain number and say he had a message from Sparrow, which was the code-word 'Hawk.' Obviously, Sparrow was code for the operative, and the FBI managed to pry out of the CIA that Hawk meant that he'd been captured or killed."

There was silence for a moment, before the Admiral continued. "As you can imagine, the message set off even louder alarm bells at the CIA, and I'm told off-the-record that the President's National Security Advisor instructed the CIA Director to do what should have been done in the first place: enlist the FBI's help in getting us to investigate. A request along those lines came to both our services and was copied to the PMO[5], who advised the Prime Minister and granted approval for a small, joint team to go in and discover what happened to the senator and CIA operative, if possible, and in any case to get to the bottom of what's going on up there.

"The Deputy Commissioner and I want you two to be a part of it. I don't know whether the fact that you're now married to each other changes anything, but you've each been highly successful at unusual assignments in the past, both on your own, and when you've worked on them together." He paused in order to gauge our reaction.

I looked over at Don. He didn't say anything or visibly react, but there was a gleam in his eye that I understood very well.

"Is that what you meant when you said joint team – police and military intelligence?" I asked.

"Not entirely," Uncle George smiled. "Our American friends naturally want to be in on this too. The idea is to have you two – and Silver, of course – from our side, matched up with two representatives from the American side. The FBI want to send Special Agent Rule. Partly, no doubt, because she also has worked well with you two before so you know and trust each other." He shifted a bit uncomfortably in his chair.

Here it comes, I thought.

"In comparison, the fourth member of the team," he cleared his throat, "will be somewhat of an outsider. The CIA will be sending one of their operatives. At this point we don't know who it will be. So that's it. I think we've told you essentially all of what little we know." He looked at Don and I in turn.

"Will you do it?"

I turned to face Don again. He was still keeping his face carefully neutral, but the sparkle in his eye was still there and as he looked into mine, he slowly winked. We both turned back to face Uncle George and the admiral and said, in almost perfect unison, "Yes Sir."

"Fine, fine," said Uncle George. I could imagine him rubbing his hands in anticipation of getting the operation underway. "As of now, you're both relieved of all other duties. You'll have until tomorrow morning to hand-off anything current to others. Staff Sergeant Blunt will serve as your point of contact. You'll have to figure out a way of maintaining communications when you're in the field, and he'll act as a relay for new information any of us may be able to obtain. He'll also be responsible for getting you whatever you may need operationally, including additional team members if you need them. Choose wisely, but in principle you potentially have access to anything either of our two countries can provide in terms of intelligence and police and military assets. Once the four of you have met and discussed it, you can choose your own leader. Any questions?"

"When will that be, Sir? I mean, when and where will we meet Vivian and the CIA operative?" I asked.

"They'll both be on tomorrow's morning flight from Washington. I suggest you meet them at the airport and take it from there."

***

The next day found us waiting at the airport when the morning flight from Washington landed. Scanning the passengers as they entered the terminal building, it was quite a while before Vivian came in. It was Silver that spotted her first, of course. As his ears perked up and he rose from his sitting position, he gave a yip and looked up at me.

"Yes, Silver, it's Vivian. Let's go meet her." Vivian was brunette, a bit taller than I am and more slender, with large brown eyes. Her manner wasn't always serious, but she tended to be very aware and intent. *The kind of person that doesn't miss much*, was my first impression when we'd first met five years earlier, and experience had confirmed that impression. We'd all worked with her before and become close in the process, so it was a warm reunion. As she knelt down to hug Silver, I asked whether she'd met the CIA operative before.

"No," she replied. "I don't even know who it is, only that the operative will have been briefed on us and should have been on the same plane."

"Isn't that taking secrecy a bit far?" asked Don.

"You'd think so, wouldn't you? But there's a lot of paranoia and the 'need-to-know' doctrine has become so embedded in the CIA's culture that we often joke that they don't even tell themselves everything they know.

"Seriously, they've had some nasty security breaches over the years, and our two agencies haven't cooperated with each other much since the '60s[6]."

"Great. Whomever this is could turn into a big liability if they're the sort that isn't willing to work with us," I grumbled.

"I've had the same thought, but they're not all cast in the same mould. I've met a few that I would trust to have my back when the going gets tough. We'll just have to wait and see."

As we watched the last of the passengers from Vivian's flight come into the terminal, we were about to give up when a man near the very rear of the crowd broke away and began walking in our direction. The first things I noticed about him were his curly dark hair and beard. His hair was long enough to project out from under the beret he was wearing, and his beard was quite bushy. Beyond that, he was deeply tanned, dressed in a tee-shirt, faded jeans and sneakers, and had a backpack slung over one shoulder.

As he continued walking in our direction, a few more things become clear. I was surprised to see that he appeared to be quite young. *Not teenager young, but not into his thirties yet either*, I thought. Given his manner of dress, he could pass for a graduate student at almost any university. *Correction*, I thought as the silk-screened image on his tee-shirt came into focus. It was Che Guevara[7]. This fellow could pass for a counterculture activist at any college or university. He even looked a bit like a young Guevara.

As he approached, Silver was staring at him intently. With my hand on his shoulder, I could feel that he wasn't sensing anything dangerous, so I assumed it was curiosity. Still, I would have liked to have known what his first impressions were.

When he was close enough for us to speak without having to raise our voices, he stopped, looked at each of us in turn and said "Special Agent Rule, Sergeant Houston, Major Harrison, and Silver. I've read up on each of you, and it's a pleasure to meet you in person. I'm going to be known as Richard Cooper on this expedition. Please call me Rick."

We responded in turn, with greetings, handshakes, and invitations to refer to us as Vivian, Alex, and Don, respectively. He had the relaxed, friendly manner of a mature university student, but there was no mistaking the intent look he gave each of us when we shook hands.

"The usual protocol is to avoid trying to pet a police dog but, since we'll be working together is it alright for me to introduce myself to Silver?"

"Yes. Just don't make any sudden movements until he gets to

know you," I replied, surprised and pleased that he would think to ask first.

He grinned. "Might take a bite out of me and ask questions later you mean? I'm not surprised. I bet he can look quite fierce when his fur is up too."

"You got that right. He nearly scared the life out of me when we first met: I thought he was a wild wolf at first."

"Ah, but now you're famous, aren't you Silver?" he said as he knelt fully down on both knees, lowered his head in a submissive gesture, and then gazed directly at him.

Silver, for his part, gave him that penetrating stare that I knew so well, and held it for what seemed a long time but was probably only about twenty seconds.

"He's reading me like a book. Isn't he?" Rick said to me without taking his gaze away from Silver.

"Probably," I said. "What did you mean about being famous?"

Rick reached out and gave Silver a gentle rub on one ear, while Silver surprised me by not only accepting it but leaning in to enjoy it. Rick looked around, but the crowd of deplaning passengers had disappeared and there was no one nearby. He looked up at me then. "Not famous in the usual sense, but famous in some parts of the intelligence community. I understand that you've met Captain Emilis Matulis, Assistant Military Attaché at the Soviet's embassy here?"

I nodded.

"I've read up on your adventure together. Must have been a surreal partnership for you, but a great success. Anyway, reading between the lines, I bet he told you that the Soviets have an entire program on ESP: extra-sensory perception?"

I nodded again. This was all supposed to be secret, but there seemed to be no point in trying to deny it, and I suspected he was partly testing me as well.

"So they do, and so do we[8]," continued Rick. "I've read both files, and there's a section in each of them on Silver, together with estimates of his abilities. I imagine that MI6 and others are at least aware of the high points." He leaned back and stood up then. "What do you think, do I pass?"

I smiled. "Let's see." Dropping to one knee, Silver immediately turned to look at me. "What do you think of him?" I asked, looking directly into his eyes.

We can't literally read each other's thoughts, of course, but the image that formed in my mind was interpreted by my brain as: *I like him.*

I gave him a pat on the head and stood up. "I think you've been accepted on probation," was all I said.

"Works for me," he nodded, seeming satisfied. "I'm probably not what you were expecting?"

"No," said Vivian. "I've only met a few operatives from Langley and they were all older and very inconspicuous-looking."

"Yes. That's kind of our standard. People that can fit into any kind of crowd without being noticed. They tend to be kind of stuffy and uptight. Sometimes I get partnered with colleagues so that our adversaries focus on me and I lead them on wild goose chases while my colleague does the real work unnoticed."

"Dangerous," put in Don.

"Very," he said with a big smile. "I think I've become addicted to adrenaline."

"So. If you're the CIA's black swan, does that mean you're not strictly need-to-know either?" asked Vivian, doing a little probing of her own.

"Sometimes yes, sometimes no. I understand the principle and I know why it's important, but it's no substitute for intuition and independent thought."

That got a rise out of all of us.

"Isn't that an unusual attitude to have in a secretive, para-military organization?" I asked.

"It is," he said, flashing another brilliant smile. "That's probably why I'm always on the edge of being fired and my boss calls me the biggest pain in the butt in our section."

I couldn't help but laugh in surprise, which had everyone staring at me. "That's exactly what my Captain used to say about me when I was on the Metro Toronto force many years ago and, in a way, it's what led to me joining the RCMP[9]."

"And have you changed much?" he asked, looking shrewd for a moment.

"Not so you'd notice," said Don before I could reply.

"Did your outfit and appearance cause you any trouble with Customs and Immigration?" asked Vivian.

"Like suspecting me of being a revolutionary or even an anarchist you mean? Not really. It did prompt the officer to ask about me politics. I said that I only wear this get-up because it helped me meet girls on campus."

"And they bought that?" I asked.

"You could say that. The officer laughed and wished me luck."

There was some shaking of heads, a pause, and then Vivian brought the meeting back to order.

"Well, Rick. Welcome to the pack. What do you say we get started?"

"Grruph!" said Silver.

Being a cautious bunch, we spent the afternoon at RCMP HQ in a meeting room that was regularly swept for bugs – electronic eavesdropping devices, that is.

First, we compared notes to ensure we were all working from the same information. Rick had been able to discover the name of the pilot that had taken the first CIA operative to the camp on Lake Athabasca, so that gave us one good lead.

Vivian had been able to interview the missing Senator's widow, and from her learned the identity of the friend that had referred the senator in the first place. From the friend, she had learned that the specific medical treatments for which he and the senator had gone there were radiation treatments. "Given the remote location, and the fact that it's probably not even on the power grid, I suspect they have an unlicensed radiation therapy machine up there," she concluded.

"I wonder where you'd get a thing like that," I said. "You wouldn't want to leave witnesses or a paper trail, so maybe you'd either try to buy one on the black market or else steal one yourself?"

"We have people that follow the black market," said Vivian. "I can make some calls."

It was agreed that she would make her calls, while I checked on the possibility of a stolen radiation therapy machine, and Rick and Don would make some calls in an attempt to locate the pilot.

CPIC, the Canadian Police Information Centre[10], was housed in a nearby building so, rather than calling them, I walked over thinking that I'd be able to more clearly describe what I was looking for if I was there in person.

One of the databases maintained by CPIC covers things that have been reported stolen, like vehicles, boats, or bicycles, for example. When I got there, I waited for someone that could help me and explained what I was looking for. When the operator accessed the appropriate database and typed in some keywords, the mainframe computer delivered the search result in less time than it had taken to explain my request. Having thanked him, I had a smile on my face as I walked back to our meeting room.

When we next gathered to compare notes, everyone had news. Don and Rick had discovered the name of the air-charter service in Fort McMurray, Alberta, for which the pilot worked. At first, this seemed like an odd place from which to book a charter to fly to the Uranium City area, but Don explained that at slightly more than 360 km (225 miles), Fort McMurray was actually the closest city to the Uranium City area, not Prince Albert or Edmonton, each of which was nearly twice as far away at 730 to 765 km (about 450 to 475 miles). Rick added that his lost colleague would have gone in under-cover and might have chosen a charter service from a different province to reduce the risk of having his cover blown. In any case, it was agreed that someone should travel to Fort McMurray and interview the pilot in person.

Vivian reported from her experts that there were no medical radiation therapy machines on the black market and probably never would be due to their size, complexity, and need for specialized, periodic maintenance. There were however, people that would be willing to steal one for a fee but that fee would be so high that it would probably be more cost-effective in the long run to simply buy one legitimately so it would have maintenance support.

My news was that CPIC had an entry for the reported theft of a prototype medical linear-accelerator called an Amelior-8. It was stolen the previous November 9, from a semi-trailer at a truck-stop about an hour's drive south of Barrie, Ontario. The machine was built in Mississauga, and was on its way to the Toronto General Hospital for evaluation and clinical trials. "I phoned the manufacturer, a company called Accelerated Nuclear Inc., and they explained that this thing was a fully functioning production prototype. They say it can deliver focused beams of either X-rays or electrons over a range of energy levels. Their claims to fame are that the machine is the most compact ever built and that it is completely automated. A computer does all the work. All a person has to do is aim the thing at the target area, key-in the treatment requirements for the computer, and then the computer takes it from there. They say the machine is worth a million dollars."

Don gave a whistle. "That's serious money all right."

"And convenient," said Vivian. "All packaged up on a semi-trailer ready to go. You steal it, take it some place out of the way, set it up, and it can almost run itself. All you'd need is a physician with flexible ethics and patients willing to pay big money to skip the waiting lists[11]."

"That and a source of power," said Rick, "but a remote site would already be on diesel power. Worst case scenario, you just buy or steal another generator for it."

"So, we may have an unlicensed physician operating a stolen, unlicensed, radiation-therapy machine to treat rich cancer patients that are in a hurry. If that's the case what happened to the senator?" I mused.

"We talked to the senator's family physician," said Vivian. "The cancer wasn't life threatening, in fact they'd already operated to remove the cancerous tumor in his upper back. The radiation treatments for which he was on a waiting list were simply to kill any remaining cancerous material. So if he died when he was at the camp, it seems unlikely that it was from natural causes."

"Maybe there's a problem with the radiation machine then," said Don. "It's a prototype after all, and you said it's computer controlled. Maybe it sometimes breaks down, or goes out of alignment, or the computer doesn't work properly, or something."

"Could be," said Rick. "If it was something like that, then they'd have known that the senator would be missed, and that there was a chance someone could have found out where he'd gone. Just the possibility would have made them extra suspicious of strangers like my colleague."

"Right, and since he was sent in to investigate…" said Don.

"Yes. He'd have had a good cover story but he would eventually have begun to snoop around," agreed Rick. "If they caught him snooping somewhere he shouldn't have been, in the middle of the night, say, and without a plausible excuse, then they might have decided on direct action. I think I should go find this pilot and see what else we can learn from him. They'd have had to make some excuse to get rid of him, and in any case, he should be able to tell us something about my colleague's cover story and the size and layout of the operation."

"Did the company say anything about the computer that runs this machine?" asked Vivian.

"Oh yes, they were very proud of it. It's a PDP-11," I said, consulting my notes, "and they said that it not only controls the machine, and the radiation dosage levels, but it takes care of all the safety checks as well."

"So," said Rick with a snort, "an almost completely roboticized medical treatment machine, and only a prototype, meaning that it basically works in the lab but hasn't been demonstrated in a real-world situation yet, or even in regular, repetitive use I'll bet. Call me old-fashioned, but that sounds like an accident waiting to happen."

That brought a few chuckles.

"Rick, you're the youngest one in this room. Are you telling us that you're afraid of computers?" asked Vivian.

"I'm not afraid of them when they're doing actuarial calculations for insurance companies or keeping track of financial accounts for banks, but putting them in charge of people's safety makes me nervous. Look, how many of us took computer science in college or university?" Everyone put a hand up. "OK, so we all know what they can do. Do you all remember how many lines of code we had to write to get the computers to do pretty simple things?" Everyone nodded. "And when we did our programming assignments, how often did the computer stop running part way through executing the programs we wrote because of some stupid little error or typing mistake?"

"All the time," I volunteered. "Sometimes, I'd have to fix an error, re-run the program until it stopped when it hit a later error, fix that, re-run it, and so on and so on, twenty times before the program would finally execute to completion and produce results. Even then, it didn't always produce the right results because of another error that didn't stop the program from running but which made the computer do something I hadn't intended."

"Exactly," said Rick, "and I bet we all worked on programming big, mainframe computers. Right?" Nods all around. "So now imagine a radiation machine that can send a high-energy beam or electrons or X-rays into your body, but it's completely controlled by a new generation small computer, and that computer hasn't been tested on any real patients yet, much less the number of patients that would have to be clinically tested before regulatory approval is granted." He paused, to let that sink in. "Now then, how many of us would be willing to take a chance on this new and unproven machine if our cancer wasn't immediately life-threatening and we had the option to wait six months or whatever and get it treated by a fully-tested and proven machine in a real hospital?"

No hands went up.

"Of course, even if you're right, the people going up there might not know that its unproven," I said.

"I'm sure you're right," said Rick. "And maybe I'm wrong about what's really going on up there."

"Maybe the machine is fine and the doctor is unlicensed," said Don.

"Maybe they're using the machine for some kind of completely new and experimental procedure," said Vivian.

"Who knows?" agreed Rick. "But it must be something like that or there'd be no need to set up in secrecy in such a remote location."

"That brings us back to something we probably all had in mind to begin with," said Don. "We'll need to get someone in there to find out what's really going on."

I was about to make a suggestion when I noticed that Vivian had been waiting for an opportunity to speak. "Vivian?" I asked.

"Yes. I have an idea," she said with a cunning-looking smile.

"This is difficult to talk about, but some time ago I had a bout of breast cancer and had to have a lumpectomy operation to remove the malignant tumor. The cancer has been in complete remission ever since, but…."

"You're suggesting you go in as a patient?" I asked.

She nodded. "That's what I propose, yes. I thought of this when I was interviewing the Senator's widow and when I interviewed the friend that had referred the senator in the first place. The friend was upset and angry, and I had no trouble getting him to agree to make a referral for me too, should it become necessary for me to go in undercover. The arrangements are made through a kind of agent in Uranium City, and I asked him to make the referral for me as a contingency. If we don't want me to go in, it can easily be cancelled."

"Don't you need to show medical records for that?" I asked.

She nodded. "I also took the precaution of having a copy of my medical records and X-rays adjusted by a radiologist consultant that the Bureau often uses. The records now show a recent test indicating some re-appearance of the cancer in some nearby lymph nodes, and the senator's friend will advise the agent that I'm both widowed and wealthy enough to pay."

"Please don't take offense at this, but are you up to the challenge?" said Rick. "This won't be a routine undercover surveillance operation, and you know what's likely to happen if you're found out…" he raised his eyebrows meaningfully.

"Thanks, but unless someone has a better idea, I don't see how else we're going to get someone on the inside. I've also been thinking that there are a few adjustments that can make me appear a little older in ways not easy to detect. That should help me avoid suspicion. If the physician is 'old school,' and if I turn on the rich-widow-charm he'll never suspect a woman anyway…"

As the day wore on, we brainstormed on other sneaky methods that we could use to reconnoitre the area and to infiltrate the camp itself, but no one came up with a better idea than Vivian's and we decided not to land on any more specific tactics until we'd learned more.

It was decided that Rick and Don would fly out to Fort McMurray and interview the pilot, while Vivian, Silver and I would fly to Edmonton and establish a staging area. We figured that it would be a lot closer to the Gunnar mine site than Ottawa but not close enough to be seen and potentially remembered by anyone from the fly-in camp on Lake Athabasca.

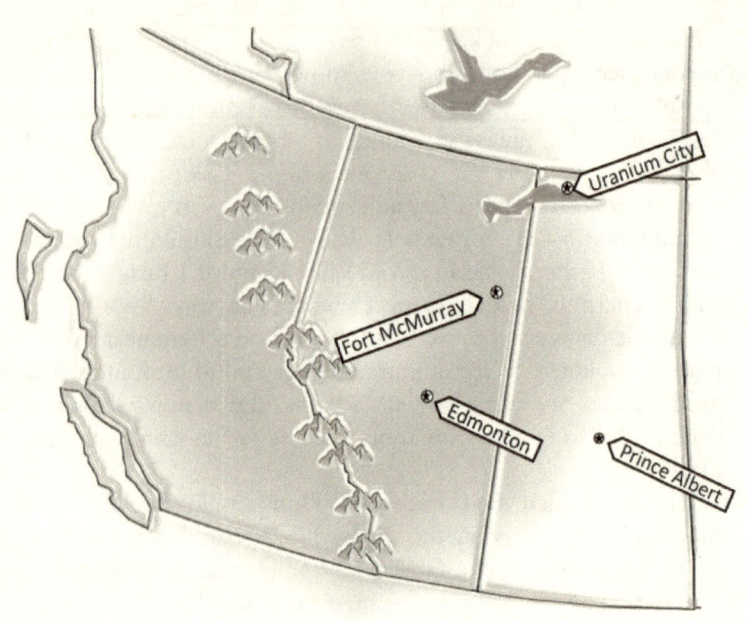

3 RICK GETS INSERTED

Friday, July 30, 1982

As planned, Vivian and I flew to Edmonton to set up our base of operations at K Division headquarters, where we were given two offices and a small, nearby meeting room to use.

Meanwhile, Don and Rick had flown to Fort McMurray to track down the pilot that had flown the original CIA operative. As they later related to us, they found him almost immediately, lounging between flights at the air-charter service for which he worked. Don identified himself with his military police ID and said he was conducting a sensitive national security investigation. That seemed to be enough for the pilot, who was happy to tell them what he could.

The pilot said that his passenger identified himself as Robert Johnson, a government conservation officer, and had said he wanted to conduct a surprise inspection at the Gunnar fly-in fishing camp on Lake Athabasca. Johnson hadn't been very specific, but he hinted that he was looking into reports of illegal moose and black bear trophy-hunting on the part of some of the visitors that were ostensibly there to fish. Johnson hadn't shown him any kind of official identification but was in uniform and the pilot hadn't had any reason to doubt his identity.

The pilot said that he been contracted to pick up Johnson in Prince Albert and fly him to Athabasca Outfitters, a fly-in fishing camp that was based out of the former Gunnar uranium mine site on the north shore of Lake Athabasca, which is what he had done. They had crossed the big lake without incident, landed on the water and taxied to the old Gunnar dock, which was showing its age but still serviceable. They were met by one of the camp's fishing guides, who used a handheld radio to call someone who seemed to be the boss, and owner, of the outfit. The boss identified himself as a retired doctor, Dr. Ernst Wildersbach, and the pilot gave Don and Rick a description of him.

According to the pilot, Johnson gave Wildersbach a slightly different description of his reason for visiting, in this case calling it a routine, surprise fisheries and wildlife compliance check. The pilot assumed that this was to avoid making them unduly concerned. Johnson said that he wanted to glance over the whole operation, and Wildersbach offered to provide a guide for this purpose. Johnson agreed, and then claimed that he'd arrived much later than planned and asked whether they could be accommodated for the night and do the inspection the next morning. This was a surprise to the pilot, who had picked Johnson up at the pre-arranged time and delivered him to the camp exactly on schedule, and who had personally made a reservation for the two of them to stay in bed-and-breakfast accommodations in Uranium City that night. Despite his surprise, the pilot said he'd kept his mouth shut and simply followed Johnson's lead.

"They put us up in a small two-bedroom house that was still in pretty good shape. It had power, but I could hear generators running so I think the whole site operation is powered by diesel generators," said the pilot. "When we were alone, Johnson said he'd pay me extra and we were always going to be staying somewhere overnight anyway, so I was quick enough to agree.

"When they drove us to our house, we drove by a small cove where the original mining company had built a small dock and even made a sandy beach. The cove was reasonably sheltered and I later moved the aircraft there for the night. I did notice that there was another aircraft there, a Twin Otter[12]. It was well moored and looked like it hadn't been flown in a while.

"After we'd had supper, we returned to the house we'd been assigned. Johnson told me was going to 'watch' for a while and not to be surprised if he disappeared for an hour or two during the night. I could tell he was up to something, of course, but he reminded me that I was being paid extra not to ask too many questions. Then he did a funny thing that made the whole situation seem even stranger. He told me that if anything happened to him, I was to remember that I knew nothing about him, and that they might tell me some kind of story aimed at getting me to fly out without waiting for him. In that case, I was to accept everything they said and simply fly out. Then, when I got back to 'civilization,' I was to phone a toll-free number he'd given me and give them a bizarre message."

"Yes," said Rick, "he told you to say that you had a message from 'Sparrow,' and that the message was one word: 'Hawk.'"

"That's right," said the pilot. "That's exactly what he said, and then it all played out just like he said too. He never did return to the house, and the next morning I pretended to have slept through the night and not to have heard or noticed anything. Wildersbach himself came to tell me that Johnson had risen early and one of the guides had taken him out by boat to tour the other fly-in fishing camps in the area, that he'd be gone several days, and that I should go ahead and fly home. He would arrange to get a message to me when he wanted to be picked up again. Well, I wouldn't normally have accepted that at face value, but since it was almost exactly what Johnson said might happen, I went along with it and flew back here to Fort McMurray. When I got here, I made the phone call, exactly as he'd asked. What the hell is going on over there?"

Don jumped in at that point, saying "That's what we're trying to find out. There's something odd going on there. Johnson was sent in to snoop around and now he's disappeared. That's why we're here. We want to find out what's going on and what happened to Johnson."

"That's not the whole story," said the pilot.

"No. It's actually hardly any of the story," laughed Don, "but it's all that is safe for you to know. Can you give us a description of each of the people you saw there?"

He did so.

"Thanks. Is there anything else you can tell us?"

"I can do better than that, I can show you." The pilot reached into the lower drawer of a desk and removed a thin zippered document case.

"Johnson left this behind on the aircraft. I didn't mention it when I phoned because he told me to stick to the words that he'd given me, but I did open it later. It shows the whole site."

Taking Don and Rick to a chart table, he opened the case and withdrew a thin set of papers and began spreading them out. "The big one is just the standard hydrographic chart of the area. You can see where the camp is here on the Crackingstone Peninsula." He pointed to the location. "Now, the others are more interesting. These drawings show the layout of the entire mine, mill, and townsite at the time when it was operating, and it looks like they were made by the Gunnar Mining Company itself."

"Can you show us which buildings seemed to still be in use?" asked Don.

The pilot pointed to the warehouse building by the dock, the house in which they'd slept, the dining hall and the hospital. "Those are the only ones I can be sure of," he said. "You can see that the house we were in was quite close to the dining hall."

"Can you tell us more about the dining hall?" asked Rick.

The pilot described what he remembered, saying that it seemed to be the same dining hall from the original mining operation days, rustic, but cleaned up.

"Any idea how many staff working there?" Rick continued.

"In the dining hall you mean? Looked like just the one cook. In the wall between the eating area and the kitchen, there was kind of a full-length open window with a broad ledge along which the various platters and bowls of food were placed. The cook was able to fill and arrange them from the kitchen side and we, on the other side, were able to go along it with our trays, selecting the food we wanted. I went up to it several times, and I only ever saw the one cook doing everything. When we were leaving, we took our dirty dishes and cutlery back, and it was still just the one guy washing up the dishes by himself."

"Can you describe the cook for us?"

"Middle-aged, grizzled, prematurely balding. Looks a bit like the stereotype of the ship's cook on a fishing boat or tramp steamer, but I have no idea whether he's ever been one."

"Did you talk to him at all?"

"Not really. He explained what was on the menu when we first arrived. That was simple as there weren't many choices available: one main, a couple of choices of vegetables, a couple of salads, bread, and so on. Then, when we brought our dirty dishes back, I asked if he'd like a hand cleaning up but he said no, that there wasn't much to do and he was going to finish it up and then go visit the 'Angler' for a drink. By that he meant the Northern Angler camp, which is another fly-in fishing camp that is quite close-by. I've flown people there myself many times. Anyway, from the looks on the faces of two of the guides that were sitting nearby, I took that to mean he was a regular drinker over there. Some of the fly-in fishing camps have a reputation for a bottomless open bar, which means they get visited a lot by some of the locals in the area. The most notorious is the Northern Angler which, as I said, is quite close to the Gunnar site where the Athabasca Outfitters camp is."

"How do they communicate with the outside world?" asked Rick, "radio?"

"That's right," said the pilot. "Some of the camps are just on Marine VHF and they get messages relayed by other boaters and other camps in the area. Some of them though, like the Angler, have a ham radio base station from which they can cover a greater distance, but they still rely on messages being relayed, or telephoned, by other ham operators."

"Can you connect to them?"

"We can call the ones with ham radios directly, yes. For the others we have to go to ham operators that also have Marine VHF, which is most of them, and get our messages relayed. Why?"

"Can you call up this Northern Angler Camp and see if they have room for a guest?"

"Sure, for when?"

"Soon. Tomorrow even. And for at least a week, if possible."

The pilot agreed to try and went off to the charter company's radio room. When he was gone, Don asked Rick what he was thinking.

"I'm thinking that I could go in now and do a little drinking with the cook from Athabasca Outfitters – the one we're interested in at Gunnar."

"Intel gathering?"

"Sure, but I'm thinking that if he's a heavy drinker it wouldn't take much to make him get a little sick too." He grinned.

"Hmmm. You mean it would be quite a coincidence if he was too sick to go back to cooking at the camp for a while."

"You're quick, Don, I'll give you that."

"OK. Suppose he happens to become temporarily incapacitated. That gives us a chance to substitute a cook of our own, but who? And how would we get one up there in a hurry?"

Rick's smile turned crafty. "It would be me, of course."

"You? You realize it would mean commercial-style cooking for whatever number of people happen to be in the camp?"

"Sure, but you're looking a man of many talents." Rick gave him a boyish grin. "At one time, in my notorious youth, I was a cook on an ocean-going trawler. That meant feeding about twenty people or so but spread out across the six watches[13]."

Don shook his head in wonder. "Talk about having hidden depths. Are you sure you want to take the risk?"

Rick nodded his head. "It's kind of why I'm here. It's not so much that I was picked to come – I volunteered."

"Volunteered? You somehow strike me as ex-military, and you know what we say about volunteers?"

"Someone who misunderstood the question?" He laughed. "Well, you're right. I spent some time as a Ranger in the army.

His grin vanished. "Before I was recruited to the CIA, I was in the military and each of our services has a version of 'leave no soldier behind, dead or alive.' You Canadians probably do as well." He looked at Don, who nodded. "Well, the man calling himself Johnson was a colleague and a friend. He may not be alive, he may not even be up here, and even if he is we may not be able to rescue him, but someone has to try."

"I get it," said Don, putting a hand on Rick's shoulder. Well, the only question now then, is whether the fishing camp is fully booked or not."

They didn't have long to wait before the pilot returned, saying "You're in luck. They're not actually very busy right now so they'd be glad to have a paying customer show up on short notice. They're still on the air so if you come with me, you can give them your name and a credit card number to hold your place. Then, I can fly you in tomorrow, if you like."

"Sounds like your cue all right," said Don as Rick got up to go with the pilot.

When the booking had been completed, Rick and Don huddled to clarify their next steps and it was agreed that Rick would leave the next day for the Northern Angler Camp, from which he would try to infiltrate the Athabasca Outfitters camp at Gunnar. Don, for his part would fly to Edmonton, bring Alex and Vivian up to date, and work with them on their own means of getting to the area.

Assuming that Vivian was able to get in as a patient, they would try to have her bring a concealed radio of some kind to give to Rick.

"OK," said Rick. "We don't know what she's going to look like when she gets there, possibly similar but older-looking, so let's agree on some simple recognition words: 'Cat' for me, 'Mouse' for Vivian, 'Dog' for Alex, and 'Guns' for you."

"Fine. We'll see if we can find a way to insert Vivian as well, and Alex and I will be lurking somewhere close by, but you're going to be on your own out there for a few days."

"Situation normal," smiled Rick, "but if I can get in, I'll keep a low profile and gather what intel I can until Mouse shows up."

The next day they flew out, but in different directions, with Don flying southwest on a commercial flight to Edmonton, and the charter pilot flying Rick northeast to the area of the two fishing camps. In Rick's case, it was only about an hour's flight and when they were close, he was able to have the pilot circle over the Athabasca Outfitters/Gunnar site so he could enhance his mental map of the layout, then on to the Northern Angler Camp.

At the latter camp, Rick threw himself into the role of 'just another American customer.' In contrast to the university student/rebel image he'd portrayed when flying to Ottawa, he was this time playing the dedicated fisherman. While in Fort McMurray, he had had both his hair and beard cut fairly short, and he had acquired typical outdoor adventure clothing including a couple of lightweight, ripstop-nylon[14] shirts, long- and short pants with cargo pockets at the thighs, and a baseball cap sporting the logo of a famous brand of fishing gear. In this guise he was accepted at face value, checked-in, assigned a comfortable room, given a tour, and was able to arrange to go out fishing with a guide in the afternoon.

The fishing was good, partly because the local guides knew all the best locations, and Rick returned with several lake trout and northern pike. He'd been quite proud of one 42-inch (1.1 m), 36-pound (16 kg) lake trout in particular until the guide told him about the largest one ever caught in Lake Athabasca: which weighed-in at an incredible 102 pounds (46 kg)[15]. Nevertheless, he'd had an enjoyable and productive outing consistent with his cover story, plus the luxury of having the guide clean his fish and even package and freeze them for him.

The camp's dining room was like everything else in the camp:

nice but rugged rather than luxurious. The food, on the other hand, was great, and Rick lingered over his meal so he could eavesdrop on the conversations among the other guests.

Near the conclusion of the meal someone stood up to welcome the recent arrivals, like himself, and to remind them about the lounge and games room and that the bar would close at 11:30 pm.

Rick divided his evening time between exploring the camp facilities, walking along the dock and shoreline, and making the occasional foray into the lounge and games room to check for non-clients. The only people that ever seemed to be in the latter were clients, however, so he eventually gave up for the day.

Patience is a virtue, he thought to himself, although it was not a virtue that came easily to him. The next day comprised an early morning fishing trip to a different location than he'd been taken to the day previous. This time he was able to catch several arctic graylings. The afternoon brought another trip to yet another fishing spot, where he was able to catch several walleyes. After spending most of the day out on the water he was famished when it came to suppertime, which comprised another great meal featuring fresh fish one of the guides had caught that day. After eating, Rick went for a walk around the camp and spent some time just sitting outside looking out across the lake, before wandering over to the lounge and games room for a look around. A quick scan of the inhabitants produced only the recognizable faces of his fellow guests, so he casually walked back outside and resumed his seat by the camp's dock.

As a beautiful, peaceful evening descended he was just beginning to doze off when he heard the sound of a motorboat approaching.

Finally, Rick thought.

In due time a boat arrived at the dock. It looked very much like the ones already tied up nearby, except that this one was painted in the different colours and had the name Athabasca Outfitters stencilled near the bow. A grizzled, older man climbed out of the boat and Rick had time to examine him while he was busy securing it at the dock. The charter pilot had been able to give him only a general description of the Athabasca's cook, but Rick was reasonably confident that this was be the cook in question.

"Howdy," said the man when he'd straightened up, turned toward the lodge and caught Rick's eye. "Get out fishing today?"

"Sure did," enthused Rick. "Caught a couple of nice-sized lake trout and a couple of respectable northern pike!"

"Good for you," said the older man and, with a friendly nod, he walked over to the main lodge building.

Meanwhile, Rick made a show of dozing off again although he was in no danger of falling asleep any time soon. He was going to give it some time before making a move. In fact, it was more than an hour before Rick judged that it would be entirely normal for a tired customer to head for the bar before turning in. When he did enter the lounge and games room, he spotted the grizzled older man sitting alone at a small table in the corner that was quite quiet as a consequence of being as far away as possible from the part of the room where most people were playing games and chatting.

Rick made a show of walking by the various games that were being played and then sauntered over to the corner table.

"Mind if I join you? It's quieter over here," he said, giving a meaningful tip of his head toward the games area, then he reached out a hand to shake. "My name's Rick Cooper."

"Be my guest," was the reply. "Alistair Hughes. You're the fellow that caught the fish." It was a statement rather than the question, but Rick answered anyway.

"That's right, although I have a feeling that everyone that comes up here catches fish."

"Pretty much. At least the ones that want to." He went ahead and answered the question that was obvious from Rick's expression. "What I mean is, some people just come up here to get away and relax. Oh, they might go out with the guides once in a while, and even go through the motions of fishing, but they leave just as happy whether they catch anything or not."

"I hadn't thought about that," said Rick, truthfully, "but I guess that makes sense. Me, I'm here to fish and relax, but in that order. How about you?"

"Not me. I don't catch them, I cook them."

"You buy them, you mean?"

"Well, that too, but what I mean is, I'm the cook at the other fishing camp. The one that's just around the peninsula from this one."

"Really! The cook. Been working there long?"

"Just since the beginning of the season. They only just opened over there."

"Well, it's a small world. I worked as a cook once – for a year it was."

"You don't say. Where was that?"

"Let me go get a drink and I'll tell you about it." After getting up, Rick turned back before leaving the table. "What are you drinking? I'll get you fresh supplies."

The camp had an open bar that was tended by one of the fishing guides. "I see you've met the competition," he said when Rick approached, but there was no malice in his tone or expression.

"Alistair? I guess so. Says he's the cook over at the other camp. He must like your camp better than his."

The guide snorted. "More like he likes our prices better. We have an open bar, even for the locals that drop by, but he has to pay for his drinks at his own camp. Our management thinks it's good policy to have the locals feeling kindly disposed towards us and it livens the atmosphere up somewhat."

"He's a regular then?" Rick asked, as if guessing.

"Oh yeah. He's like the definition of a regular. Be careful if you decide to have more than one or two drinks with him – he's apt to get boisterous when he gets drunk."

"I'll bear that in mind. Thanks," said Rick, borrowing a tray on which to put the four drinks he'd ordered, two for himself and two for the cook.

Returning to the table, Rick passed over the drinks and explained about having spent a year as ship's cook on an ocean-going trawler.

"Better you than me," said Alistair. "I get seasick just being out on the lake here when the weather gets rough. And it's worse when I've been drinking."

Rick looked pointedly at Alistair's empty drink glasses that had been pushed to one side on their table.

"Why do I do it then, you're wondering?"

"No, no. I'm far too polite to ask," he said with a smile.

"Well, I'll tell you anyway. The pay's good, but there's nothing else up here to do. Someday I'll pack it in and go somewhere else, but I need to save up some money first."

Rick nodded. "Makes sense. It was the same with me and my ship's cook job. After a year was up, I'd saved almost everything I'd been paid and went on."

"What did you do then?"

AN INVETERATE MOUNTIE

"Well, there's a story there. I didn't want to get another job as a cook so I changed direction completely and…" Rick went into a lengthy description of his next job, how he'd landed it, and some of his experiences. It took some time, because it was quite an adventure and, perhaps surprisingly, he told the complete truth – at least about that phase of his life.

As the evening wore on, they exchanged more stories and had several more drinks each, although Rick always volunteered to get them so Alistair was unaware that, early on in the evening, Rick had switched to non-alcoholic drinks for himself.

When the bartending guide announced Last Call for drinks at 11 pm, Rick went to the bar to get one last nightcap drink for each of them. While there, he unobtrusively dug a small prescription-pill bottle from his pants pocket, tapped out a small, white pill and pretended to pop it into his mouth. "Touch of sinus congestion," he said to the guide. "Came on when I was flying in this morning."

When the guide turned to serve another customer, Rick dropped the pill into Alistair's drink. It dissolved almost immediately. As they finished their nightcaps and continued to trade stories, Rick watched Alistair with heightened interest. The latter was already flushed and sweating to some degree, but these were both enhanced within about fifteen minutes. When the announcement that the bar and lounge were closing, Rick got up from his chair saying "I could use some fresh air before bed anyway – I'll walk you down to the dock."

"Sounds good," said Alistair who rose rather unsteadily, then quickly made a grab for the back of his chair. "Must have had a couple too many. I'm feeling dizzy."

"Do you need a hand?"

"No. I'll be fine once I get to the boat."

As they walked to the dock, Alistair's gait was slow, unsteady, and erratic and he was beginning to feel nauseous, so he was in no condition to notice that Rick didn't seem at all intoxicated.

"You feeling OK?" asked Rick at one point.

"No," said Alistair with a groan, and clutching his stomach. "I think I'm going to be sick. It's strange. I haven't gotten sick from drinking since I was a kid."

"Maybe you've caught a flu bug or something," said Rick sympathetically.

When they reached the Athabasca Outfitters boat, Alistair bent down to untie the mooring rope and immediately dropped to his knees and violently threw up the entire contents of his stomach. Although almost everything was vomited right away, he continued with dry heaves for some time, then collapsed to a sitting position on the dock.

"Whew," he gasped. "I don't think I'm going to be able to survive the trip back."

"Tell you what," said Rick, in a concerned voice. "I'll take you back. Just give me a minute to go tell one of the guides so they know what's happened to me."

Alistair just nodded and remained sitting while Rick jogged back to the lodge. When we returned a few moments later, he found Alistair in the same position, with his head down, and moaning.

"OK. Will you be able to direct me if I drive?"

Alistair nodded and Rick helped him into the boat then got in himself, pushing off from the dock as he did so. The motor started up immediately, and they headed out. The Athabasca camp wasn't far away, but as they progressed out of the relatively sheltered water near the Northern Angler camp it became increasingly clear that the weather had worsened while they'd been drinking and the lake had become quite choppy. As they made to round the point of the peninsula, they were even more exposed and the swell had their little boat hammering into one wave after another.

This is going to make him feel even worse, if that's possible, thought Rick to himself, and indeed, Alistair was huddled on his seat with his head down and his hands gripping the boat, still retching with dry heaves.

Once they'd rounded the point, Rick could see the massive headframe[16] from the old Gunnar mine and he simply headed in that direction until Alistair waved one arm and pointed to the small marina where they should dock. When they neared the small dock, Rick shut off the motor, clambered over Alistair, and grabbed a mooring ring. Then he got out of the boat, tied it up, and reached down to help Alistair out of the boat. Even in the dim light he looked paler than he had when they left the other camp.

As they walked up the slope from the water, everything was quiet. Rick could hear a generator running somewhere, and there were a couple of makeshift streetlamps on which provided just enough light for them to see the roads and structures. Rick had to hold onto one of Alistair's arms now for him to be able to walk, and the latter used the other arm to give directions to his house.

About halfway there, they encountered a man that Rick guessed was one of the camp guides. He took one look at Alistair and laughed. "Well, you must have outdone yourself tonight, Alistair!"

"We met in the bar at the Northern Angler camp," explained Rick. "I think he's got something more wrong with him than drinking too much. I don't think he'd have made it back if I hadn't brought him."

"OK," said the man, pointing to one side. "His house is right there. If you wouldn't mind helping him get there, I'll go get the boss – he's a doctor."

"Sure. I'll wait." Rick helped Alistair to his house, where the latter collapsed into a living-room chair.

It wasn't long before the man returned with an older man that he introduced as Dr. Ernst Wildersbach, the owner of the camp. Wildersbach had brown eyes, dark hair, thick eyebrows, mustache, and a short Van Dyke-style beard.

Must have to dye his hair to keep it that dark, thought Rick, as the doctor began checking Alistair over while at the same time asking him about his symptoms. When this was done, he stepped back and gazed thoughtfully at Alistair.

"What do you think doctor?" asked Rick.

"I'm not sure. No. Not sure at this stage. The nausea and vomiting, stomach pain, weakness and dizziness suggest possibly a stomach flu or food poisoning, and he's flushed and sweating but he's not running much of a fever. He might have the Norwalk virus[17]. He says that he didn't eat anything when he was over at the Northern Angler?"

Rightly taking this to be seeking confirmation, Rick answered. "I don't think he did. Not while I was with him anyway."

"Hmmm. Well, the virus can be spread by either food or person-to-person contact. Embarrassing for us if he caught food poisoning from his own food, but no one here has reported feeling unwell yet. Time will tell."

"A virus and a severe hangover. I wouldn't want to be in his place tomorrow morning."

"Tomorrow morning. My God! Someone has to cook breakfast for our guests and staff!" He turned back to face Alistair. "What about it. Do you think you'll be up to cooking breakfast tomorrow?"

"Arrrgh," said Alistair, who was holding his head in both hands. "I wouldn't count on it." Then he looked up, wincing in pain from the sudden movement. "The way I'm feeling, I may not even survive the night.... Maybe you could get Rick here to cook for me for a while – he's been a ship's cook."

As the doctor turned to look at Rick he summarized his experiences as a ship's cook, repeating the essentials of what he'd told Alistair earlier in the evening.

"A year as a ship's cook you say, and for a crew of twenty?"

"About that. Sometimes a few less, sometimes a few more."

"Hmmm." The doctor took a long, thoughtful look at Alistair, who looked worse, if anything. "Why don't you stay on here overnight. It's much too dark for you to go boating in unfamiliar waters. In fact, I'm surprised you made it here without incident. No. No. I think you should stay here in one of our guest houses for the night."

Rick made a show of hesitating. "Well...."

"It's the least we can do to show our appreciation for your Good Samaritanism."

Rick made a show of considering the offer, then shrugged. "I am kind of tired so, OK, I accept. Thank you."

"Fine. Fine. Let's Alistair into bed, then come with me and I'll take you to one of our guest houses."

As the two men walked to a nearby cluster of small houses, Wildersbach said, "You know, I'm not at all sure that Alistair is going to feel up to cooking tomorrow. What would you say to staying on here for a day or two and take over the cooking while he recovers?"

"Work here you mean?" said Rick, in a surprised voice.

"Yes. Yes. But just for a day, or two. It would help us out tremendously, and when you're not busy in the kitchen, you can still get out with one of our own guides and boats and get some of the fishing done that you came here for." Seeing that Rick was considering it, he added "We'd pay you of course. We wouldn't expect you to work for free. If you don't mind my asking, what kind of money were you making as a ship's cook?"

"Oh. Well, when I first started, I was getting $4.50 an hour, but by the time I'd been doing it for a year I was getting $9."

"How about if we consider it like overtime and pay you double:

$18 an hour?"

"Canadian or American?"

Wildersbach smiled. "I meant Canadian, but I'll pay it in American if you'll do it. What do you say?"

Rick hesitated, then seemed to come to a decision. "All right. I'll do it. But only for a couple of days, OK?"

"Fine. Fine. Here we are at a house you can use. Why don't you go inside and relax for a moment. You'll find a complete set of fresh linens and towels and things inside." He stepped back and looked at Rick consideringly. "We should have something that will fit you well enough. I'll have someone bring you some toiletries and a change of clothes. After breakfast tomorrow I'll have one of our guides take you over to the Northern Angler so you can get your gear."

Within an hour, Rick was settled into bed for the night.

Good old '796[18], he thought as he drifted into sleep. *Works every time.*

Rick rose early the next morning, made his way to the dining hall and looked everything over. The kitchen was well laid out and well stocked, so he put a large urn of coffee on the percolator and began assembling things for breakfast: juices, fruit, breads, and jams, etc. There were toasters on the dining-room side of the broad serving window so people could toast their own choices of bread, and there was a selection of cereals for which he put on a large urn of hot water to heat for those that wanted porridge. For the hot dishes, he began preparing hash-brown potatoes and, while these were cooking, he started on sausages and bacon, all of which would eventually be placed in large warming trays and put out to sit along the serving window. When people came in to eat, he planned to cook them eggs to order as they went by the serving window.

Everything went well, with Rick constantly having to answer questions along the lines of 'What happened to Alistair?' It was near the end of the breakfast period when a nurse came in to ask for a breakfast tray for their new patient.

"Sure," replied Rick. "Do you think he's up to eating solid food this morning?"

The nurse made it very clear that no, she did not, but that it wasn't up to her. The doctor wanted him to try.

"OK," said Rick cheerfully. "How about juice, dry toast, and some fruit for now? If he can keep that down, I can supplement it later."

The nurse though that would be entirely appropriate, and waited while Rick assembled a tray. As he handed it to her, he said "I just put on a fresh urn of coffee to perk. When it's ready, I can bring him a cup if you like?"

She thought that would be fine, thanked him, and left with the tray.

Rick really had just put on a fresh urn of coffee that he'd planned to keep available for people for the rest of the day. When it was ready, he poured a large mug two-thirds full then made up the rest of the volume with brandy from a bottle he'd discovered in the kitchen's huge pantry. After that, he dropped in one of his little white pills.

When he'd carried the steaming mug of coffee to the small hospital, he asked the nurse if he could take it to Alistair himself so he could try to cheer him up, and was told that would be fine as long as he only stayed a moment. Thanking her, he went to the room she indicated.

"How are you feeling today? Any better?" he asked, as he entered the room. It was set up with two beds but Alistair was the only patient.

"Not worse anyway," Alistair grumbled. "Slept like a log, but woke up with the world's worst hangover!"

"Did you eat any of your breakfast?" Rick asked, casting a glance at the food tray, which was obscured by a crumpled white napkin.

"Not much," was the reply. "Don't like fruit but had a sip of the juice. Tasted terrible! I did eat the toast, but only to make the nurse shut-up and go away."

Rick chuckled appreciatively. "How about some nice hot coffee? I just made it fresh."

When Alistair seemed to hesitate, Rick immediately placed the forefinger of his left hand alongside his nose and said, "I think you should try it. It's my own special coffee."

Alistair's eyes brightened immediately as he guessed Rick's meaning and he reached out for the mug. After taking a first, cautious sip, he took a second, deeper drink, then sat back against his pillow and gave a contented sigh. "Rick, you are a lifesaver!"

"Best cure for a hangover," Rick whispered confidentially. "But not a word to anyone or I'll never be able to bring you another one."

Alistair responded by taking another sip and them mimicking Rick's finger-alongside-nose gesture, saying "Just between us cooks."

"Fine," said Rick. "I'll come back and check on you a bit later. Who knows, you might need another coffee."

Rick had been back in the camp kitchen for perhaps twenty minutes when Dr. Wildersbach came in for a cup of coffee. Rick was just on the verge of striking up a conversation with him when the nurse ran in saying "Doctor, he's vomiting up his breakfast." As the doctor went out with the nurse, Rick went back to cleaning up the kitchen and dining room. A passerby would have heard him whistling while he worked.

When Rick returned to his accommodation that morning, he found that his duffel bags had been retrieved from the Northern Angler camp and were there waiting for him. Taking them into the bedroom, he very carefully opened each one, paying particular attention to the clothes piled at the tops. Then he stepped back and looked out the window for a moment. It was Rick's habit to always place strands of coordinating-coloured thread on top of the articles in his bags so he could easily determine whether they had been searched in his absence. In this case, the threads were gone.

Well, well, he thought. *Not a very trusting bunch I'm staying with! Good thing I didn't bring anything incriminating with me.* He reached into his pocket and brought out two amber-coloured[19] prescription-pill containers. *Except these, of course.* But he wasn't worried about the pill bottles. In addition to the standard size, shape, and colour of the containers themselves, they each had authentic-looking pharmacy labels giving the names of himself, the prescribing doctor, and the pharmacy. The label on the bottle containing the PP796 pills indicated that the pills were captopril, a common blood pressure medication that was normally formulated into small white pills that looked very much like the ones in Rick's container. The second pill container had a similarly authentic-looking label but contained a very different kind of pills.

I'm in! thought Rick. *Now all I have to do is lie low, keep Alistair in the hospital, keep my eyes and ears open, and wait for Mouse to show up.*

It was Tuesday, August 3.

4 VIVIAN GETS INSERTED

Meanwhile, two days earlier (Sunday, August 1)
Edmonton, AB

Our plan was to have Don and I pretend to be research scientists doing some kind of fish-health or limnological research[20] on the lake, which would give us an excuse to loiter around in the waters near the Athabasca Outfitters camp.

In this regard I had contacted Dr. Alan Grey, my old analytical chemistry professor at Carleton University (where I had originally trained as an analytical chemist) and asked if he would 'hire' me back as a Research Associate, and then send me out to Northern Saskatchewan to collect the appropriate samples for a fictional research project. He knew about my current job and, in fact, I'd done something like this once before, with his help, and it had been quite effective[21]. Just like before, Dr. Grey found the idea quite amusing and said he'd be glad to play along in this latest 'cloak and dagger' affair of mine. With his help, we decided that I'd go out to collect samples for a study of possible connections between radioactive metal concentrations and tissue health in the Lake Athabasca fish population. All Don and I would have to do was catch samples of the fish species, dissect them, and freeze them in sealed bags that could be shipped back to the university for analysis. So, it was settled that Alex Houston, B.Sc. would re-enter the world of science for a while.

Dr. Grey had also agreed to contact a chemistry-professor colleague of his at the University of Alberta (U of A), whom he knew well enough to ask for the use and/or donations of an appropriate collection of lab-ware, reagents, and sample bags and bottles. Accordingly, Vivian and I had taken an unmarked police SUV and driven to the U of A Chemistry Department.

There, Dr. Grey's friend had assigned a research associate (who managed her lab for her) to guide us around and help us find what we needed. We did far better than I'd expected, and came away not only with the lab- and sample-ware I'd asked for but also the loan of a stereo microscope and a compound microscope[22].

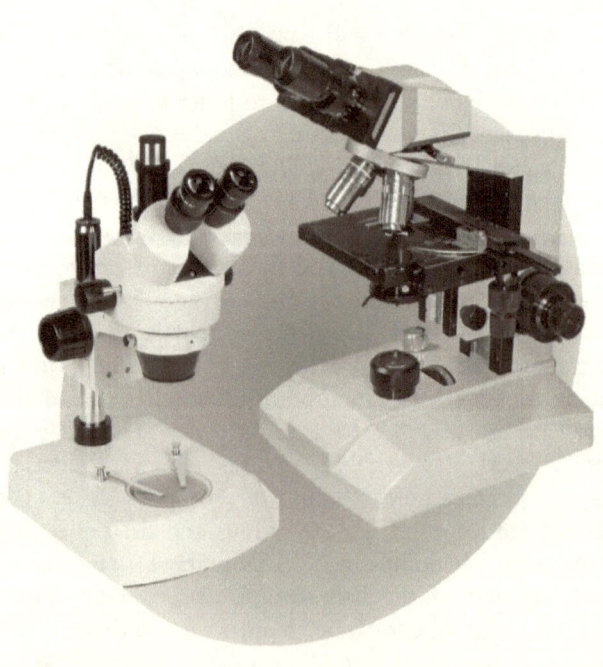

For communicating with each other, I had signed out five Motorola MX300 hand-held VHF radios plus a base station, all of which had crystals for the standard and tactical frequencies, plus the relatively recent feature of DVP voice encryption[23]. The base station was to be installed on whatever kind of boat we were able to rent for use on Lake Athabasca.

Beyond that, we had a lot of shopping to do, but most stores were closed on Sundays, so we had to wait a day[24]. At mid-day, I drove to the airport to pick-up Don, who was flying in from Fort McMurray. On the way back from the airport, Don summarized what he and Rick had learned from the charter pilot and explained about Rick seizing the opportunity to fly straight to the fly-in fishing camps and attempt to infiltrate the Athabasca Outfitters camp. When we got back to our temporary office space at K Division headquarters we were in for a surprise.

When we walked into our meeting room there was an older woman waiting for us, dressed for the wilderness with a kind of safari-style outfit comprising khaki shirt and pants, low hiking-style boots and a bush hat. Don and I stopped in our tracks for a moment, but Silver just calmly walked up to her to smell her clothes and accept a pat on the head. I did a double-take in the same instant that I realized why Silver was being so friendly.

"Vivian! I hardly recognize you," I said, looking her over. "You've dyed your hair grey and done it up in a bun, and under those old-style cats-eye glasses your eyes look grey too. Contact lenses?"

Vivian nodded. "The contacts change the colour and they also make me near-sighted. The glasses don't change my colour, but they correct my vision back to normal. That way if someone picks up my glasses and looks through them, they'll appear real. There are some distortions though, so it's a bit disconcerting to have my vision change twice like that, but I'm getting used to them."

"Very ingenious," I said. "And what have you done to your skin?"

"You like it? I've tried to keep it simple and understated. I've made my face paler with a bit of light foundation and some touches of green concealer rubbed into spots on my forehead and cheeks. I've added hints of wrinkle lines to my smile line and chin using a fine brush and a darker concealer, then brushing them over with a wide brush and a lighter concealer, and using a sponge to soften the edges. It's supposed to be subtle and easy to repair and easy to reproduce each morning. Anything more exotic and the doctor might catch me out."

"You've done something else to your face too," I said, holding her at arms length and peering at her.

Vivian opened her mouth in a wide smile. "Tooth overlays that change my facial profile just a bit, and with a few imitation gold fillings consistent with being from the previous generation. They're just like dentures, really, except that my real teeth are under them."

"Amazing," said Don.

"Think it will work?" she asked.

"Well, you'll never fool Silver like this, but beyond that I think you're good to go."

Another thing we got done, despite it being a Sunday, was finding and booking the rental of a houseboat that was docked at Fond-du-Lac, a remote fly-in community on the eastern shore of Lake Athabasca. It being prime summer-vacation season we had to take the only one left, which was probably larger than we needed, but the operator explained that it was seldom rented out due to its relatively high rental rate. From the description, it sounded like there would be lots of room for us to live and also operate a modest floating-laboratory operation, and we were assured that we'd also be able to rent a motorboat we could use for fishing and sampling.

The next day, Monday, was shopping day. We had two unmarked police SUVs assigned to us, so we divided up tasks and Don went off in one while 'the girls,' Vivian and I, took the other.

For his part, Don started out at CFB Edmonton (commonly known as Namao[25]), where he signed out duffle bags filled with camping gear suitable for use on a houseboat, such as sleeping bags, a cooler for extra food, and even fishing tackle. From there he went off to grocery-shop for the non-perishable food. Fresh food we planned to purchase when we got to the lake.

Vivian and I started out at camera shops in search of used camera gear of the sort that a reasonably serious amateur photographer might carry around. We had no trouble finding a Nikon 35mm SLR camera and compatible wide angle, normal, and telephoto lenses plus film and a selection of lens hoods and filters.

It took a bit longer, however, to find a suitable camera bag that could hold all the gear and in which we could also hide the relatively bulky handheld VHF radio I had. In the end, we had to buy a brand-new one which we 'weathered' by taking it to a commercial laundromat and washing a few times on a high-temperature cycle and substituting bleach for detergent. After that, we put the camera bag into a dryer, added a pair of running shoes, kept tumbling the bag until it was not only dried but well pummelled. It came out looking respectably shabby and I later was able to take advantage of the Velcro™-tabbed dividers to create a hidden compartment at the bottom-rear of the bag in which to place the police radio. The camera and lens compartments were then arranged beside and above it. It wouldn't stand-up to a careful search, but we thought it would pass a casual one.

After that, we shopped for a few other things like disposable Styrofoam coolers for packing the fish we planned to catch for shipping back to a lab for analysis. With so much gear assembled, we had to charter a plane to fly it, and Don, Silver and I to Fond-du-Lac, where we had rented the houseboat.

On the following day we parted. Don, Silver and I flew to Fond-du-Lac, while Vivian stayed back. The next day, she would fly to Fort McMurray enroute to the Athabasca Outfitter camp as their latest patient.

***

Wednesday, August 4

Vivian had an uneventful airline flight to Fort McMurray, met the same charter pilot that had been interviewed by Don and Rick, and flew with him to Lake Athabasca. In contrast to the commercial jetliner from which she had just disembarked, the charter flight was in a Cessna 206 bush plane fitted with amphibious floats[26]. Never having been in a small airplane before made the next flight a completely different flying experience.

On the negative side, the seats were less comfortable, there was no in-flight service, and the ride was quite bumpy with a few patches of frightening turbulence. The noise would have been deafening as well, had not the pilot invited her to sit in the right-hand seat up front and provided her with a set of headphones that screened out most of the noise and allowed her to listen to the radio communications and occasionally converse with the pilot himself.

On the positive side, they flew at a vastly lower altitude than had the jetliner, so she had an excellent view of the terrain over which they flew, which was principally composed of forests, rocky patches and lakes. The pilot directed her attention forward when the huge expanse of Lake Athabasca came into view[27], and again when they were close enough to the lake to experience the amazing sight of the broad sand dunes adjacent to the southern lakeshore[28]. As they flew over the sand dunes, she had the surreal experience of feeling like she was momentarily flying over a portion of the Sahara Desert that had somehow been magically transported from North Africa to northern Canada. After that, it was almost an anticlimax to fly across the lake itself and land close to the abandoned Gunnar mine and mill site, home of the Athabasca Outfitters camp.

When the pilot had taxied to the main wharf, Vivian's introduction to the camp mirrored that received by Senator Harland Walker almost exactly two months earlier. Upon disembarking, she was met by the distinguished-looking Dr. Ernst Wildersbach.

"Welcome, welcome," he said. "How was your trip? No trouble I hope?"

"No, everything went fine," Vivian replied, "I'm just tired from all the flying. Something about air travel really wears me out."

"Of course, of course," said the doctor. "Everyone says the same thing. If you're not too tired, we'll offer you a nice hot meal and then show you to your cottage. Then tomorrow, we'll show you everything, explain everything, and after that we can get straight to your treatment."

"That's music to my ears. I can certainly stay awake long enough to eat!"

"Fine, fine. I will lead you to the dining hall and then I will have one of my assistants show you to your cottage. Don't worry about your luggage, it will be waiting for you when you get there."

"Oh yes, that reminds me. There's another fly-in fishing camp near here isn't there? One called the Angler, or something like that?"

"Yes. Yes. The Northern Angler camp is very close. Why do

you ask?"

"The charter company asked me to try to deliver a camera bag to one of their guests that they took there on Sunday – someone named Richard Cooper. Apparently, it was accidentally left behind at the airport."

"Richard Cooper. Richard Cooper. Would that be a Rick Cooper by chance?"

"I suppose so. I really don't know."

"Well, there is a Rick Cooper who is a guest over at the Angler, but he's helping us out over here right now doing temporary duty as our cook. Our regular cook has taken sick, you see, and we've been most fortunate to have Rick fill-in for us. I must say," the doctor added, in a confidential tone, "that the standard of cooking has improved as a result, so you're in for a special treat. Yes, a special treat."

"Well. That's fine then, isn't it. Let me just collect the camera bag from the pilot and we can see if it belongs to your new cook." As he did with all those who came for radiation treatments, Dr. Wildersbach led Vivian to a waiting pickup truck, they both got in, and as he drove, he gave a running monologue pointing out some of the features of the long-abandoned uranium mining operation. As they bounced along the rough roads, Vivian made appreciative sounds and comments, and before long they ended up at the original cookhouse, now renamed.

"This is our dining hall," the doctor said as they walked inside. "You'll find a meal schedule in the house you've been assigned to. The house will have a fully functional kitchen stocked with a few necessities but for full meals, everyone eats here." When they walked over to the broad, open window across which the food dishes were set out, they could see that there was a man working in the kitchen.

"Good afternoon, Rick. What's on the menu for tonight?"

"Hi Doc," said Rick, with a wave. "I'm making up a special baked Walleye. It just came in from one of the guides. It'll get lightly breaded and seasoned, then very gently baked. I'm trying to outdo those pan-fried fireside meals that the guides make for your clients for lunch out in the field. I'll be serving it with baked beans and fried potato wedges, plus a nice assortment of salads."

"My goodness, if you can better the guides, we'll never let you go! Rick, I'd like you to meet our newest arrival: Vivian Rule."

"Nice to meet you Vivian," said Rick. "Please excuse me for not shaking hands but, as you can see, they're covered in flour," he said, holding up his arms to display white, flour-coated hands and wrists.

"No problem," said Vivian. "But you might want to clean up anyway, because I brought you something." She held up his camera bag.

"My camera gear!" he exclaimed. "How did it come to you?"

While Rick went to the big sink to wash, Vivian explained about the charter air service finding it left behind. "I was going to ask the doctor whether he could radio the other camp so you could come and get it, but it turns out you're right here."

"Well that's a happy coincidence," Rick said as he walked over to the window and accepted the bag. Then he opened it, making sure that the doctor had a good view of the contents, and took out the camera body and one of the lenses. Putting the two together, he removed the lens cap and experimentally focuses on the far corner of the dining hall. "Everything seems to be intact. Not even a mouse got in! Thank you for bringing it for me."

"My pleasure. I'm glad there was no mouse. I saw a cat sniffing at the bag in the air terminal, so I wondered," she quipped, providing Rick with the second code word. "I was coming to this camp anyway, so it was no trouble at all."

"Since you have a little time before supper, I'll show you where you will be staying," said the doctor.

"See you later," added Rick, closing up his camera bag.

With a wave to Rick, Vivian followed the doctor out of the dining hall and back in to the truck. From there they drove a short distance past several larger buildings, that the doctor explained were abandoned bunkhouses, to where a half-dozen, well-spaced, small houses were located. "These have all been very nicely fixed up for our patient-guests, because they are right beside the hospital," he added. Then, having ushered Vivian into one of the houses, he handed her the key, saying "I think you will find this a bit rustic but quite comfortable. Yes, quite comfortable. I have some other things requiring my attention right now, but I may see you at supper this evening. In any case, I will come and collect you at breakfast in the morning.... You did bring the X-rays and medical report with you?"

"Oh yes, I brought everything you asked for. It's all in my

luggage."

"Fine. Fine. We'll review those in the morning and I will show you everything and explain everything, and then we will be able to begin the treatment. Tomorrow morning without fail" and, so saying, he took his leave.

After a brief rest, Vivian walked to the dining hall for supper and was surprised, intrigued, and more than usually on her guard when the doctor came to her table and asked if he could join her. She naturally agreed, and found him to be an engaging and entertaining conversationalist. Their wide-ranging conversation continued well past the conclusion of their meal, and it occurred to her that the doctor seemed to be showing an unusual level of interest in her. *Romantic interest?* she wondered. *Real or feigned then?*

When they eventually rose from the table, the doctor, who by that time had insisted she call him Ernst, invited her to go for a stroll before turning in for the night.

They continued their conversation as they walked down to the lakeshore and she showed a suitable level of interest in hearing about his career in Europe. This allowed him to brag a bit, and her obvious appreciation for his anecdotes of trials and accomplishments seemed to have the desired effect.

After sitting at the marina for a while, enjoying the view of the lake, the doctor – Ernst – walked her back to her house, thanked her for the pleasure of her company and took his leave.

Interesting but dangerous, thought Vivian, wondering which was more likely, that the doctor was playing games with her or that she had found a weakness she might be able to exploit.

Oh well, at least I made it in and met Rick already! thought Vivian. *Now all I have to do is see what I can learn and hope to survive the medical treatment.*

5 THE SCIENTISTS ARRIVE

Meanwhile, a day earlier (Tuesday, August 3)

Don and I had flown to Fond-du-Lac, in the northeast corner of Lake Athabasca, to board the houseboat we'd booked. Our float plane had docked very near to where the houseboat was tied up so that, after signing the rental and payment paperwork and borrowing a hand-cart, we were able to quite easily transfer all of our gear from the plane. It was time-consuming, however, so by the time we were finished there was just enough time to do some shopping, for which we left Silver behind on the boat.

Fond-du-Lac, is a remote, fly-in settlement of the Fond du Lac Denesųłiné (Dene) First Nation. It is one of the oldest, most northern communities in Saskatchewan having been originally established around a Hudson's Bay trading post in the late 18th century. The community's population is about 900 people, most of them of Dene or Métis descent, large enough to support a well-stocked combination grocery- and department store that was the successor to the original trading post. We were able to buy all of the perishable foods we wanted, and lingered for a while to take in other features of the store like their displays of handmade fur hats, mittens, and moccasins. There was also a very nice bakery, from which we purchased an assortment of wonderful-smelling baked goods. We were even able to buy a good supply of dry ice that we would use to keep our fish samples frozen.

After hauling the groceries back to the houseboat, we again left

Silver behind and went in search of a late supper. The community had a couple of places from which to choose. We ended up at the dining room of a lodge and were treated to a very nice homestyle meal. After that, it was late enough that we simply left the houseboat tied up where it was and spent our first night there.

Wednesday, August 4

The morning brought another travel day for us, and for Vivian as well. While Vivian was spending the day travelling to, and getting herself established in the Athabasca Outfitters camp, we set out on the lake to navigate our way westward towards Uranium City. I say navigate, and we had brought along a hydrographic chart[29] and sought advice from the locals, but all we had to do really, was to head west and follow the north shore.

Don and I took turns unpacking and setting up our gear, including creating a realistic-looking research setup, but that left lots of time to just sit and enjoy the scenery. I'd mentioned that it was a large houseboat. Officially it was listed as "sleeps 16," but it would more realistically be up to twelve if you didn't count the ability to fold-out the sofa bed or convert the kitchen table. In any case, there was lots of room for us and our gear.

We'd also rented a twelve-foot, aluminum-hull 'zodiac-style' hypalon™ inflatable boat[30] and 40 hp outboard motor. The boat could either be towed behind the houseboat or else secured on the top deck. To facilitate this, there was a swing-out boom and electric winch that could be used to (separately) raise and lower the boat and motor.

I'd never been on a houseboat before and found it very relaxing. Of course, being a large (over fifty feet, 15 m, in length) and heavy craft, its 'cruising speed' was eight knots (about 15 km/h, 9 mph). The upside was that time slowed down for us and we could enjoy the trip.

I particularly liked sitting up on the flying bridge, where there was a 360° view. The north shore featured alternating patches of tree-less rocks and clusters of black spruce and jack pine; in one place I spotted two moose placidly foraging, in another a black bear, and in still another I watched a muskrat approach the shore and smoothly slip in to the water. In the air, we spotted a much wider range of birds including several species of ducks, some loons and herons, some ruffed grouse, a couple of hawks, an eagle and, of course, quite a few Canada geese. Silver was well used to being in boats – even on this very lake[31] – so he was quite content to simply lounge on the upper deck where he too could look around.

At a speed of eight knots, it took a little over five hours to reach Uranium City, where we put in to take on fuel and spread our cover story about being biologists on a research cruise. From there, another two hours put us in the vicinity, but out of sight of, the Athabasca Outfitters camp. There are quite a few islands in the vicinity, and we picked a spot among them that was well sheltered, but neither overly conspicuous nor hidden, and tied up there for the night.

Thursday, August 5

We knew that the guides in the fishing boats would see us, of course, but we thought that it was better to let them come to check us out than the reverse. Besides, we had some fishing to do in order to add realism to our story. So, in the morning, we pulled out and anchored a short distance away to do a little fishing and Don actually caught two northern pike, which we filleted and dissected. I took a couple of samples from one of them to create examples we could put under our microscopes. I'd also cheated by purchasing some frozen fillets at the store in Fond-du-Lac to form the beginnings of our 'research collection.'

If things had gone well by this time, Rick would be in place as camp cook, and Vivian established as a patient.

We didn't think it would be very long before someone from Athabasca Outfitters dropped by to play the innocent passerby as an excuse to see what we were up to, but were surprised that it happened within hours rather than days. It was just after lunch when a fishing boat motored up to the stern, and a male voice called "ahoy there."

"Good morning," I said, when I reached the stern. I noticed, as I did so, that the boat had the name Athabasca Outfitters stencilled near the bow.

"Ben Delorme. I'm one of the guides at the Athabasca Outfitters fishing camp just over there on the mainland," he said, waving an arm in the direction of the camp. "I just thought I'd drop by to say hello and ask if there's anything you need."

"We're fine for now, but that's very good of you," I congratulated. "Would you like to come aboard for a cup of coffee?"

"That would really hit the spot," he said, and he tied up his boat and clambered out.

"I'm Alex and this is Silver," I said, as Silver approached him for an investigative sniff. He'd put out a hand to sniff, but he immediately snatched it away when Silver began a menacing growling.

"Silver!" I said, in an admonishing tone, at which he reduced his grows to a low level but didn't entirely stop. I noticed that his hackles were up a bit. "He's just trying to defend me," I said, by way of explanation.

With a wave, I turned and led the way to the galley – it looked more like the kitchen in a motorhome than a boat's galley – with Silver following along behind, still with a low series of growls that, were he human, would have been like grumbling under his breath.

"This is my husband, Don," I said when we got there.

"Ben Delorme," he said, shaking hands with Don. "One of the guides at the Athabasca Outfitters fishing camp just over there on the mainland."

"He came to see if we need anything and I offered coffee," I said. We already had a pot of coffee on the range, so I poured three cups while Don asked him some questions about how their fly-in fishing season was going.

"We have a few guests right now," he said, "but it's been slow this year."

"Are you two some kind of scientists or something?" he asked, noticing the two microscopes we had set up on what would otherwise be the dining table, and the obvious array of glassware and other paraphernalia that surrounded them.

"That's right," I said. "We're part of a research project to study the uptake of radioactive metals by the fish in the lake, especially those caught near the abandoned Gunnar uranium mine site on either side of the peninsula. We've already caught some *Exos Lucius*, that's northern pike, out here and later on we'll move to the other side of the peninsula and try to get some *Coregonus clupeaformis*, lake whitefish, in Langley Bay.

"We're especially interested in uranium and some of the elements from its decay series, like radium, and lead[32]. We're not just going to measure the uranium content, because the different radioisotopes can migrate into the environment at different rates. After we've dissected the fish, we put samples of the muscle, liver, and bones in these plastic bags and keep them frozen on ice. They'll all be analyzed later, but you can see what the tissues look like under these microscopes."

I showed him a sample of fish tissue under the stereo microscope, then a stained sample, that was mounted on a cover slip, under the higher magnification of the compound microscope.

"Very interesting," he said. "How many fish do you need for this?"

"We're trying for at least a half-dozen of each species from each location, in order to have statistically representative results when the analyses are done."

"OK. And what are you trying to prove?"

"Not so much prove as learn. We think that the tailings are virtually certain to have spilled over into Langley Bay, and that rain and melting snow will be leaching additional material and washing it into the bay with each successive season. The solid particles will be gathering in the sediment, and from there the radionuclides can get into the water, and therefore into the fish. That should mean that the fish in the bay would have greater concentrations of radioactive metals in their tissues than the same fish out in the lake proper, like where we are right now, and even those should have higher concentrations in them than fish in other lakes and rivers that are not close to uranium mine tailings[33]. Depending on what we learn, it could provide a reason for the government to begin cleaning up these old uranium sites, and it's possible that the fish aren't actually safe to eat."

"Oh. The boss won't want to hear that!"

"No. I'm sure you're right, but your customers should be fine since they'll only be taking a few fish to eat. The local residents, on the other hand, have been here eating the fish for decades since the mine and mill closed. That might be a different story."

"Oh. Well, I suppose that wouldn't be so bad then."

"By the way, do you think we could get permission to catch some samples from the flooded-mine pit? The radionuclide levels in the fish might be even higher in those fish[34]."

"I don't see why not. I'll mention it to the boss. Drop by sometime, the boss is a doctor so he might like to meet you and hear about the fish anyway."

"Thanks, we'll do that," said Don.

I walked with Delorme back to the stern of the boat, with Silver trailing us and looking unhappy, and saw him off.

"What do you think?" I asked Don when I returned to the galley.

"He probably really does serve as a fishing guide, but he has the manner of a guard, or maybe ex-military, about him. He wasn't obvious about it, but when you were explaining the scientific stuff, he took a good look at everything."

"Yes, and Silver's senses obviously had him concerned too. It's a good thing we hid the radios and base-station antenna down in the engine compartment. We might as well bring out the base station and get its antenna up. We could get a call from Rick anytime now."

The rest of our day was uneventful and we had a leisurely afternoon and enjoyed a gorgeous evening twilight over the lake.

Friday, August 6

After breakfast, we took the inflatable boat and went to Athabasca Outfitters to ask for permission to collect some fish from the flooded open-mine pit. We were met by Delorme, making us wonder whether he had been watching for us, but he was civil enough saying, "I already spoke to the boss about your request. He's too busy to come himself, but says you are welcome to go ahead. If you'd like to hop into my truck I'll drive you to the pit."

We loaded Silver and our fishing gear into the back of the truck, then got in ourselves and he took us the short distance to the flooded mine-pit. Circling around it, he drove to the far side of the pit, where the remnants of forest bordered it, and where there was a rowboat beached and tied to a large tree. He said he'd come check on us later in the day, but that he wasn't sure when that might be. We thanked him, and said we'd be fine to simply walk back to the dock when we were done.

We spent the morning out in the pit fishing. Although we fished from the boat, we didn't fish too far from shore because most of the fish we caught were from less than about 25 feet (7.6 m) down. In five hours, we caught six northern pike (*Esox lucius*) ranging between 51 and 66 inches long (1.3-1.6 m) and six common suckers (*Catostomus commersoni*) that ranged between about 30 and 46 inches in length (76-117 cm).

With the fish in hand, we rowed back to shore and beached the rowboat where we had found it. After tying it up to a metal ring that was attached to a heavy chain, we followed the chain back to where it was secured to a large tree.

"Look at this," said Don, inspecting the robustness of the method that had been used to secure the chain. The fittings were heavily rusted. "They didn't just bring the boat here for us, they've been tying it up here for some time."

When we walked back to the water's edge, we took a careful look at where we'd pulled the rowboat while pretending to be checking to make sure we hadn't left anything behind. Sure enough, there were a number of grooves on the beach showing where it had been pulled up on previous occasions.

"Why keep a boat here?" wondered Don out loud.

"I don't know," I replied. "I doubt anyone would swim or catch and eat fish from the pit that you'd have to assume was radioactive, especially when there's a massive lake within sight that's bound to be cleaner and have healthier fish in it."

"No," he said, thoughtfully, "you wouldn't want to risk taking anything out, but you might want to put something in it."

"You mean like disposing of things you don't want found, like deceased patients, you mean?"

"Maybe. Or possibly even someone that you caught snooping around just that little bit too much."

"It's an idea. I don't see how we're going to search it though. It's probably several hundred feet deep[35]."

With these chilling thoughts in our minds, we gathered up our fish and fishing gear and walked the roughly half-mile back to the dock on the lake where our inflatable boat was tied up. Once we'd loaded the boat, pushed off, started the motor, and were out on the water, Don said, "Good thing we weren't obvious about snooping around where that rowboat was."

"Oh?" I asked.

"We were being watched all right, but from a distance, with binoculars probably."

"Must have been, or else Silver would have sensed it."

"I think that must be why they kept their distance. I only noticed when we were walking back to the dock. When I stopped to tie my bootlace, I peeked back and just caught the movement of someone hiding behind the headframe."

"I'm surprised you caught them with the old shoelace trick!"

"It was probably just a fluke and I happened to glance back just when they were changing position."

"Well," I said, "we assumed we'd be followed and watched. We were right."

"Yes, but it doesn't give us any clue what they're up to here."

"No. I think that's going to be up to Rick and Vivian."

"It's nice to be out on a mission together though," he said.

"Always!" I said, which was immediately seconded by a "Grruph!" from Silver.

Well, I thought as we motored back to the island at which we'd tied-up the houseboat, *we're in place with our cover story established. Now we watch and wait.*

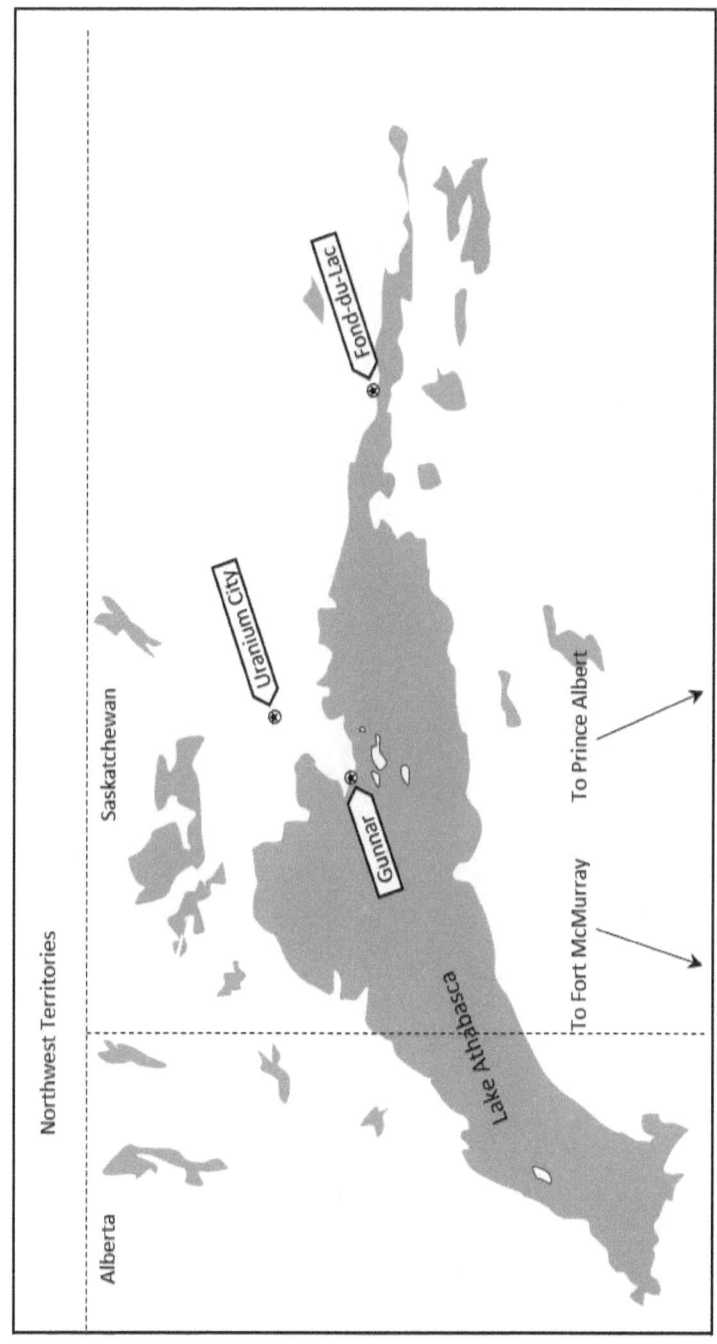

Laurie Schramm

6 VIVIAN'S TREATMENT

Meanwhile, beginning two days earlier (Wednesday, August 4)

While Alex and Don were setting out in their houseboat Rick had promptly hidden the VHF radio in the attic of the house he was staying in. Beyond that, he'd been kept busy with his cooking duties. He had also continued with his morning visits to Alistair to check on his condition and to bring him fresh cups of coffee. Although he was still adding PP796 to the coffee, he had reduced the dosage to half a pill, which was enough to give Alistair the same symptoms of nausea, weakness, and dizziness, but with less stomach pain. Plus he was able to eat some simple food, like plain toast, without vomiting. As a result, the doctor seemed to be encouraged by the apparent improvement in Alistair's condition and convinced that further bedrest would lead to recovery. Rick's aims were to keep Alistair out of commission and the doctor concerned yet content, but he was under no illusions that he'd be able to get away with it for much longer.

His role as camp cook had gone well, particularly since he tended to prepare somewhat different dishes than had Alaistair. The staff and guests had viewed this as a pleasant change and had become quite friendly except for Delorme, who seemed to be the doctor's right hand and effectively his head of security. It didn't seem like Delorme had any friends or wanted to be friendly with anyone, although Rick found him to be civil enough. After his first few days as cook, Rick had learned to distinguish between the real fishing guests and the pretend fishers who were really there for medical treatments. The former talked constantly about boats, the outdoors, fishing, fishing gear and, of course, the fish they'd caught, the ones that had gotten away, and the ones they still hoped to catch. These guests were always the first up, the first in his kitchen for breakfast, and the first to finish-up so they could get out on the water with the guides.

The pretend fishers, on the other hand, tended to sleep in, show up last for breakfast, and generally talked about anything but boats or fishing. Although, to be fair, some of them did seem genuinely pleased to be in the wilderness rather than their big cities. Rick made an effort to engage these guests in conversation whenever he could and they seemed to simply assume that, as a staff member, he must be in on the racket so they spoke to him openly when he showed interest and concern, so he had no trouble learning about their medical problems.

By visiting Alistair each day with his mug of special coffee, Rick was also able to observe where the other patients were examined and treated, although he had been careful to seem unobservant and oblivious to such things.

When he wasn't busy with planning meals, cooking, serving, and cleaning up, he alternated between going out fishing with one of the guides and going for walks around the abandoned mine site. He had even specifically asked for and been given permission for these explorations, although with a warning that some of the houses and structures might be in danger of collapse and that there were almost certainly chemical and radiation hazards in and around the mill and acid plant buildings[36]. He wasn't interested in the latter buildings, but did survey the entire site, discovering as he did so a little neighbourhood of small houses that were located some distance away from everything else at the tip of the peninsula. Among the other houses, dormitories, and buildings he learned which few were in use, another few that remained abandoned but seemed structurally sound, and those that appeared to be completely unsafe.

One of Rick's mottos was 'check your six[37],' and it was something he practised religiously. As a result, on his first two strolls around the site, he was fully aware of being followed, but he'd expected that. The man following him the first time wasn't very good at it, but Rick ignored him and played the innocent but curious visitor. The second time, it was Delorme following him and

Delorme did know how to shadow someone. Here again, Rick was careful to give no sign of being aware of his follower and stuck to his casual sightseeing plus some extended periods of just looking out over the lake. After that, even Delorme seemed to lose interest in him and he was unable to detect followers on subsequent walks, although he remained careful and vigilant anyway.

In addition to the various buildings, and their layout, Rick also explored some of the game trails that abounded in the nearby forest. On one of these explorations, he was following a game trail when it crossed an obviously human-made but long disused and heavily overgrown gravel path. In one direction it seemed to lead to the open pit mine. Curious, he followed it the other way, into the forest. Before long, he encountered a low building. His first thought was that it was an old trapper's cabin, as it was a one-room structure made entirely from squared-off, heavy baulks of wood that were joined at the corners with classic, full-dovetail notches.

The windows were boarded-up and there was a large, heavily corroded padlock on the front door. When he went up and gave the lock an experimental tug, it immediately opened together with a mini-shower of particles and flakes of rust. Opening the door showed him nothing but pitch blackness, but he had a small penlight in his pocket. The penlight provided just enough illumination for him to gingerly step inside and look around. The shack was mostly empty, but it was immediately clear that this was no trapper's cabin. Strewn around on the floor were the remnants of small wooden crates. When he picked up one of the empty crates and held it up to the light, he could read the stencilling. On the ends, it read: "FORCITE," and on the sides: "MADE IN CANADA BY CANADIAN INDUSTRIES (1954) LIMITED."

He whistled softly. *No wonder they built this shack so far away from the mine*, he thought to himself. Replacing the empty box, he began methodically search the entire shack. He was looking for any surviving sticks of forcite[38] and, if possible, blasting caps and fuses.

Beyond the old explosives shack, the only noteworthy things Rick spotted on his strolls were the repurposing of one of the old buildings for storage, the repair and upkeep of the docks, and the rowboat tied up on the flooded open-mine pit.

For some reason he couldn't identify, the flooded pit interested him. From the maps and documents obtained by his fellow CIA operative, and delivered by the charter pilot, he knew that the pit was shaped like a tall, narrow funnel. Underneath, the miners had mined underground as they continued to follow the ore body to greater and greater depths, with a maze of underground workings that had been serviced by the hoist and massive headframe. When the mining had ceased, the company had blasted the thin shoulder of granite separating the pit from the lake, causing everything to be flooded - the open pit and all of the underground workings alike. He wondered what lay at the bottom of the pit, knowing that in many such mining operations a wide range of equipment and materials would be simply bulldozed into the pit at closure; he wondered whether there were fish still living in the lake, and if so whether they had become so afflicted with genetic mutations as to be unrecognizable; and he wondered why anyone would keep a rowboat stationed there.

On one of his fishing trips with the most friendly and outgoing of the guides, he had tried innocently asking about the possibility of radioactive fish, and had been told that no one was worried about the fish in the big lake, but no one was willing to chance fishing in the flooded pit.

Other than their meeting and handoff of the camera bag, Rick hadn't seen much of Vivian beyond the level of attention he gave each of the guests when they came to the dining hall to eat. He did notice that the doctor had joined her for supper on her first night, and that afterwards the two had gone off for an evening stroll. He also noticed that on her second day, she had taken her lunch tray and sat down with the kid that always seemed to eat alone while covering his table with a mound of computer printouts. The kid had removed his headphones when she spoke to him, cleared a space for her tray, and then went beck to his printouts. Rick was amused to see that Vivian hadn't let that pass, and somehow managed to engage him in some kind of discussion.

I wonder what's so interesting that those two have gotten together, he thought.

***

Also on Thursday, August 5

Vivian began her first full day at the Athabasca Outfitters camp with breakfast, where she smiled at Rick and exchanged a few of the same kinds of friendly comments with him that she would have with any other cook in similar circumstances. Knowing Rick's true identity, she was pleasantly surprised at how good her breakfast omelet tasted and was genuine in her praise when she left.

When she reached the small hospital, she was led to the doctor's office where he greeted her, inquired about her accommodations and meals, and then got down to business. After taking some time to read the copy of her medical file, which she'd brought with her as previously instructed, he slipped the X-rays from her file onto the backlit, wall-mounted viewing and had a close look at them as well.

"Well, well, your initial treatments went very well indeed and the new appearances of the cancer in your lymph nodes are at a very early stage. In fact, I'm surprised that your specialist even discovered them, but it's well that he did so because the earlier we can catch and treat them the better the success rate."

"That's what I was hoping for Doctor, and that's why I wanted to get the treatments as soon as possible rather wait for months and let the cancer spread."

"Very wise. I think that's very wise indeed, and since you were able to come here so promptly, I'm very confident we'll have no trouble whatsoever clearing everything up in just a few treatments.

"Nurse!" he called out, and the nurse promptly came in from the adjoining office.

"Would you take Mrs. Rule to the treatment room and get things ready while I work out the course of treatments that we'll use?"

"Yes Doctor," she said, and indicated that Vivian should follow her.

It was only a few steps down the hallway to the treatment room, but they first entered the small control room where a young woman was watching someone who was working at a computer display terminal.

"This is Lisa," introduced the nurse. "She's the technician that will operating the machine. Lisa, the doctor will bring you the prescription for Mrs. Rule's treatment in just a few minutes. He'll also bring the X-rays and show you the two locations he's going to want you to irradiate."

"That's fine. Dexter here just needs a moment to print out

some more of the computer program."

As the nurse nodded and left, a male voice said "There. I'm sending the last part that I need to the printer. It will only be a minute."

It was a young male voice, Vivian thought, and, sure enough, after pressing a few more keys on the keyboard, a thin young man with prominent glasses and a shock of unruly hair straightened and then stood up. As he did so, the dot-matrix teleprinter[39] beside him began to make a metallic, mechanical sound as its print-head began racing back and forth, alternating printing lines of text from left-to-right then right-to-left. It was printing on continuous fanfold paper that was drawn up from a box on the floor, fed through the machine by a tractor-feed mechanism that meshed with holes that perforated each side of the paper. The printed sheets were fed to a basket behind the printer in which the pages re-folded themselves into a neat stack.

"Dexter this is Mrs. Rule, our next patient," said Lisa. "Mrs. Rule, this is Dexter Sherman, our computer consultant." Although she said it with a straight face, her eyes twinkled as if to communicate that she found it amusing that their computer consultant was probably only eighteen or nineteen years old. Dexter smiled, nodded, and shook hands before turning to watch his printout being generated. He was strongly introverted and not comfortable conversing with strangers so there was an awkward silence for a few moments, but the printing was soon completed and he was able to gather up the printout, add it to several other stacks of similar printouts that were strewn on the desk nearby, and left without saying anything further.

"He's a computer-nerd[40] and he's running diagnostics for us; apparently some kind of kid-genius about computers," said Lisa by way of explanation.

"Oh. Alright," said Vivian.

Lisa led her to the inner treatment room, showed her the machine, and got her settled on the treatment table. By the time that was done, the doctor had come in with Vivian's X-rays and some written notes. After greeting Vivian, he put her X-rays up on a set of wall-mounted light boxes and showed Lisa the target zones for the treatment.

"I want you to set-up for the 10 MeV electron-beam treatment, and deliver a 200 rad dose to each site."

"Yes, Doctor."

"Excellent. Excellent. Now then, Vivian," he said, taking one of her hands in his. "You have nothing to be concerned about. I will leave you in Lisa's capable hands, and I will come back and check on you in a little while."

"Thank you Doctor," she replied.

When he'd left, Lisa moved the treatment table and rotated the gantry so that the first treatment beam would be aimed where she wanted it, then said, "The machine has been aimed, now I'm adjusting the beam width so we just hit the first part that we want to be targeted by the electron beam…. There. Now, I'm going to leave the treatment room and sit down at the computer console in the next room. There's an intercom we'll be able to use to speak to each other. OK?"

"Yes thanks," said Vivian, doing her best to hide her nervousness.

Lisa went to the next room, closed the door, sat-down at her computer terminal, and switched on the intercom.

"Mrs. Rule. Can you hear me?"

"Yes."

"OK. I will provide a running commentary so you know what I'm doing out here. You just lie there and relax, and I'll tell you which times you'll need to try very hard not to move your body."

"Alright."

"Here we go. The machine and computer are on, and I am just typing in your name and the machine settings. The computer will now check to make sure that the data I entered matches the settings I just made manually when I was in there with you. It will only allow me to proceed if they match perfectly. That's for your safety."

There was the sound of clicking as Lisa pushed the keys on the keyboard. She was reading the lines as they came up on her display. Eventually, it read:

```
SYSTEM: BEAM READY      OP. MODE: TREAT      AUTO
```

"OK. Everything looks good. Hold still now." Lisa then hit the one-key command B, for beam on, to begin the treatment. There was a brief mechanical sound and then the room suddenly went black and silent. There was a squeal, but it came from Lisa rather than Vivian.

Vivian only had a moment to consider what might have happened before a Lisa came into the room waving a flashlight in front of her.

"Are you OK?" she asked.

"Yes, fine," said Vivian. "What happened?"

"Power failure," Lisa replied. "The generator probably went on the blink again. It only happens rarely, but it does happen, I'm afraid. Let me help you up off the treatment table."

After assisting Vivian, she led her out of the treatment rooms, down the corridor, and to the hospital entrance.

"Wow. It's nice the see daylight again," Vivian commented, squinting through the door.

"Yes. I have to go find the doctor and let him know what's happened. Are you OK to walk on your own, or would you like my help?"

"I'm fine now dear," said Vivian in her most grandmotherly voice, "you just go on about your business and I'll go back to my house. Do you think the power will be out in the dining room too?"

"It should be fine. The hospital and dining room are on separate generators."

"In that case, I think I'll just walk over there and get myself a nice cup of tea."

When Vivian entered the dining hall, it was empty except for some sounds emanating from the kitchen and one table in a corner that was completely covered with heaps of computer printouts with Dexter buried in the middle of it all, alternately holding up sheets of fanfold paper to read and making notations on a pad of paper.

She first went to the kitchen's serving window. "How's our master chef doing this morning?"

"Oh, hi!" said Rick, looking up from where he'd been crouched by a low cabinet searching for some kind of cooking utensils. "I'm doing just fine, thank you." He rose, walked over to the window, and looked around the dining area to see who was there, then in a low voice said "I couldn't help noticing that you met our new computer consultant."

"Dexter? Yes, we were introduced just this morning when I went for my first treatment, and we had breakfast together."

"Ah. I'm not supposed to know about the medical treatments, but there aren't many secrets from the staff around here. How did it go?"

"It didn't. There was a power failure just when it they were about to start. Everything's on hold now until they find out what's wrong and get the generator fixed. They're expecting to have it back on this afternoon."

"Umm hmmm. Are you a betting woman by chance?"

"Me?" she said, surprised. "Well, within reason I suppose. Why?"

"Because I'll bet you it doesn't get fixed quite that easily. I happened to be walking by the hospital this morning and noticed that the generator sounded a bit rough and was producing quite a bit of smoke."

"And?"

"And I wondered whether it might have a bad batch of diesel fuel in it."

"Is that common?"

"Well, it happens, you know. There could have been too much water or sludge in the tank, someone might have mistakenly topped the tank up with gasoline instead of diesel, that kind of thing."

"You seem to know a lot about it."

"Not really, I've just picked up some little bits of experience here and there over the years," he said, putting on an innocent expression.

"Hmmm. Remind me never to play poker with you. I don't think I'll bet against you now either. OK then, smarty-pants, how long do you think it will take them to fix the generator?"

"They might have some mechanically-minded people in a camp like this. I'd say tomorrow afternoon at the earliest."

"Sounds like someone has either accidentally or deliberately bought me a little time then."

Vivian had been fixing herself a mug of tea while talking. As she made to walk away, she lowered her voice even further, saying, "Glad you're here Rick."

Rick smiled and reached over to put a small dish of fresh doughnuts on her food tray. "All part of the service."

Walking over to where Dexter was seated, Vivian noticed once again that he had a lightweight pair of headphones on. Judging from the sounds, he was listening to some kind of noisy music.

Realizing that he'd never hear her if she said anything, she simply pulled out a chair and sat down right across the table from him.

He saw that almost immediately, sat up and looked at her while lifting the headphones from his ears. That made the type of music, at least, quite clear.

"Heavy metal?" she asked, looking meaningfully at the headphones.

He blinked. "Yes," he said, looking confused.

"Well don't look at me like that. I may be old but I'm not dead!" She smiled. "Black Sabbath?"

"How do you… I'm sorry, I mean yes, it's called *War Pigs*[41]."

"Good choice," she said, then smiled again. "Do you mind if I join you?"

"Uh. No. Not at all," he said, looking up and blinking a few times through his glasses. Then he switched off his Sony Walkman and set it, and the headphones, aside then pushed some of the printouts to one side so there was room for her tray, which she was still holding. In doing so, a few piles of paper from the far side of the table slipped of and fell to the floor but he didn't seem to notice. In fact, he immediately put his head down and returned to his reading of printouts and making notes on the pad of paper.

Vivian studied him over the brim of her mug of tea. Her first and second impressions of Dexter were that he fulfilled most of the stereotypical characteristics[42] of a computer scientist: male, pale and thin, wearing glasses, probably very intelligent, obsessed with computers and programming to the exclusion of other interests, lacking interpersonal skills and socially awkward.

"May I ask what you are doing?" she said.

"Me? Oh. You mean with all this?" he looked up and pointed to the piles of printouts. "Debugging."

"What does that mean?"

Dexter paused in thought for a moment, as if considering how to phrase an answer she could understand. Then he pushed his glasses higher on the bridge of his nose. "They think there's a problem buried somewhere in the computer program. Sometimes when they tell it to have the machine use a certain energy level or duration, it doesn't do it."

"You mean it refuses?"

"Oh no. A computer can't normally refuse a program instruction. It's more like it doesn't turn the beam on, or not high enough, or not for long enough."

"So in that case the patient doesn't get the treatment. Why were they going to treat me this morning then?"

"I think it's because it doesn't happen very often. They told me that it almost always follows the commands the operator types into the terminal, but once in a while, like maybe one time in twenty, say, it doesn't do it."

"I see," said Vivian in a thoughtful voice. "Does it ever go the other way then?"

"The other way?" Dexter sounded confused.

"I mean does it sometimes turn the beam on too high, or for too long?"

"Oh. I'm sure not. They would have told me, wouldn't they?" He sounded horrified. "I mean, they wouldn't keep treating people if that were the case. I mean, do you know what could happen to a person if the energy level was really cranked up?" If possible, he looked even more horrified, as the implications took hold in his imagination. Then he seemed to get a grip on his thoughts and shook his head. "No. I'm quite certain they would have told me."

"I'm sure you're right," she said, not believing it, then tried changing the topic slightly. "So what are you doing about this 'bug' as you call it?"

"I'm going through the computer program line by line so I can figure out what the original programmers have done. It's not really all that complicated, but as you can see," he waved at the piles of printouts, "there are an awful lot of lines of code – I mean many, many lines of text giving the computer instructions."

"Yes, I can see that," she said, bending over to peer at some of the typed lines on one of the pages. "How did you ever learn to do this kind of thing and where did they even find you? There can't be all that many people around that can do what you're doing."

"I don't even know for sure," he said, thoughtfully. "Someone came to one of the meetings of a computer club I belong to at Stanford. It's where a bunch of us computer hackers get together to learn about the latest developments in computers and to talk about our projects."

"Projects?"

"Right... ah, do you know what a hacker[43] is?"

"I think so. Someone that builds or modifies their own computers or writes their own computer programs?"

"Exactly!" he said, sounding relieved. "In my latest project, for example, I designed a telephone interface board that plugged into one of the expansion slots on my computer and allowed me to interface with the phone system and generate phone company tones. Then I wrote a program that made my computer do the dialing and search for phone numbers that had computers attached to them. It was fun, but then a friend of mine that had done essentially the same thing carried it too far and had his computer making over a hundred calls an hour. That got the telephone company upset, and when he started using it to find WATS[44] numbers, with which he could make free long-distance calls, he not only got in to more trouble with the phone company, but the FBI too[45]. That's when I started being a lot more careful in what I was doing."

"The FBI you say? Yes, I can imagine that might be scary," murmured Vivian.

"Right. I wasn't trying to do anything wrong. It was just the challenge, you know?"

"I do know. So, someone came to your club you were saying?"

"Oh, right. Yeah. This guy came and said they were acting as the agent for a company up north that needed someone to go up and debug a computer program on a PDP-11 computer. It would be a summer job, they said, with good pay and room and board included. I needed a summer job but hadn't quite gotten around to doing the applications, and we were already into summer, so I put up my hand."

"And here you are," said Vivian. "Are you enjoying it?"

"Oh yes! Their problem isn't easy to diagnose so it's fun, and also good experience for me. If I succeed, then I might be able to get a similar job back home…. By the way," he said, shifting the subject abruptly, "is it weird that they're paying me in cash?"

His question caught Vivian off guard, but she recovered quickly. "I don't know about weird. It's unusual, certainly, but it's not illegal."

"OK. That's good."

"And how are doing in your debugging task?"

"Well, it's complicated because there are sometimes a lot of things going on at almost the same time. For example, there are bending magnets that are used to shape the beam and once the instruction is given it takes about eight seconds for the machine to move the magnets to where they're supposed to be so a flag is set to indicate that's happening. During that time, the computer is busy doing other things, so it has to go back once in a while to see if the flag has been cleared. Then it has to check to see if there are any other change requests, before moving on to the next task. Does that make any sense?"

"I suppose so. What's the problem?"

"I don't know yet, but there's only a limited amount of memory available to store information and there are a lot of things to keep track of, so the programmers made a whole bunch of these logic sequences, and a whole bunch of assumptions. Then, based on those, they wrote a whole set of user instructions so that the user would only type in certain instructions, in a certain order, so that none of the assumptions would be violated."

"And?"

"And everything looks fine! I mean, if you do what the manual says to do, and in the sequences that the manual says to use, then the program works and the machine does exactly what it should."

"So what are you working on now then?"

"Well, I'd asked Lisa to tell me everything she could about what she'd done differently each time there'd been a problem and she said nothing. But then I sat in on some treatments she was doing and I noticed that she'd developed a way to quickly make changes when she entered something wrong. She uses the 'cursor-up' key to edit the entry, then, instead of re-entering all the other treatment information, she just hits the return key over and over again to get back to where she was before. That leaves all the other values unchanged."

"OK, is that a problem?"

"Well, you wouldn't think so, would you? I mean the terminal screen will show that all the entered values look correct, but that's not how the manual says to make changes, and I'm wondering whether doing it her way violates some of the assumptions the programmers made about how long it takes for the mechanical tasks."

"Like moving the magnets you mentioned."

"Right. So I'm trying to imagine I'm the computer, and Lisa's making her quick changes, and I'm trying to change beam energies and move magnets to keep up with the instructions I've been given."

"I can see why you're having to concentrate so hard. I think I'd better stop distracting you so you can get on with your work then, but thank you for explaining it to me."

"You're welcome," he said, looking directly at her and blinking a few times. "You know, you're the only person that ever asked me about it."

"Tell you what. If I see you again tomorrow, I'll come and ask you how you're doing."

When Vivian left the dining hall, she went for a short walk that took her behind the hospital, which enabled her to observe a man on his knees and bent over part of the large generator that was located by the back wall of the building. He seemed to be dismantling part of it. Based on the number of components lying on the ground beside him, and based on the stream of swearing and muttering she could hear, the process was not going well.

Smiling to herself, she continued on to her house, where she changed clothes and then went back out, this time to explore around the abandoned mine and mill facilities.

At supper that evening, the doctor once again came and asked if he could join her.

"Of course, Ernst. Please do," she replied. By tacit agreement, they referred to each other formally when in the hospital but were otherwise on a first-name basis.

The doctor began by apologising for the disruption caused by the failed generator and confidently predicted that everything would be back in working order by the next morning. Vivian allowed herself to be soothed and they were soon discussing other subjects.

Once again, the doctor invited her for an after-dinner stroll and they walked along a different route this time, one that took them away from the larger buildings and in the opposite direction from the mine and mill facilities. This took them along an old road that was obviously not often used, and culminated in an unusual scene at the end of the peninsula.

"What do you think of this Vivian?" he asked.

"Why, it's like a little suburb!" she exclaimed, taking in the series of quaint, small houses that were arranged there, each with its own front and back yards – although small ones – and most with the bent and rusting remains of children's swings and toys in their yards. "They even have little white picket fences around them. These must have been for the families."

"Yes. The more senior staff were allowed to bring their families with them. It would have been a way of encouraging them to come and work in such a remote area, I imagine. And you can see that they've located them where there are very nice views of the lake, and as far away as possible from the mining operations."

"It's beautiful."

"Yes. We'd have fixed up some of these houses for our little camp except that it's better for us to be close to the dining hall and hospital and, of course, the docks and so forth."

They walked to the water's edge and stood for a moment taking in the evening view over the water.

"You could almost imagine yourself retiring to a place like this," said Vivian.

"You think so?" asked the doctor, startled. "You really feel that?"

"Yes I do Ernst, why the surprise?"

"Because I feel that way myself. Yes I do. And you're the first person to come here and react the same way. The fishing fanatics come to fish and relax for a while but then rush home. The medical patients come here to hasten their treatment, and then they want to rush back to their normal lives. The staff are here for the money, and only the money. Even our fishing guides are tired of fishing and tired of having to deal with our guests. But I...."

"Yes, Ernst. What about you?"

"It's so different than anywhere I've been before. I feel that I could stay here – live here – even if we shut down the business and everyone else left...."

"Wouldn't you become lonely Ernst?"

"Yes. Probably so. Probably so. There are people around though. Nice people really. And interesting. They've all come to get away from something, but they share an attraction for living in such remote and peaceful country. Of course, if I had someone to share it with...."

"Like me you mean? Isn't that a little sudden Ernst? We've only just met you know."

"Yes. Yes. Of course. I apologise. I wasn't meaning to rush you or anything. It's just that it feels so natural to be talking to you about anything, and I feel that I can relax when we're together.

Well, you know what I mean."

"I like you too Ernst," said Vivian. "But let's not rush things, OK?"

"No. No. Absolutely not. But I do wonder. Vivian, your treatments are not going to take very long, and I'm expecting complete success. Yes, complete success. And after that, you'll be flying back to wherever home is."

"Virginia."

"Ah. Virginia. I've never been there. Well. Well, after you've returned home would you permit me, that is, could I come and pay you a visit some time?"

"I think that would be very nice Ernst. I will make sure you have my phone number and mailing address before I leave."

The doctor lapsed into a contented silence, and they automatically began retracing their walk back to the house in which Vivian was staying. After saying their goodnights, the doctor moved on and Vivian stood in her living room for a moment, reflecting. *Well, well,* she thought. *It's been a long time since I played the part of a siren on a case.*

Friday, August 6

At breakfast in the morning, Vivian ordered another omelet and when Rick came to the serving window to hand it to her, he said "Careful, the plate is just a bit warm."

Reaching out to take the plate, she detected what felt like a piece of paper underneath so she was careful to place the plate on her tray in a way that didn't dislodge whatever it was. As she walked across the dining room, she held the tray firmly with her left hand and used her right to explore under the edge of the plate. There was a piece of paper there. As she walked, she slipped the paper into her hand, crumbling it up as she did so. When she'd selected a table, she put her tray down and strolled over to the ladies' washroom.

Alone in the washroom, she opened up the paper and smoothed it out. On it was written a brief note:

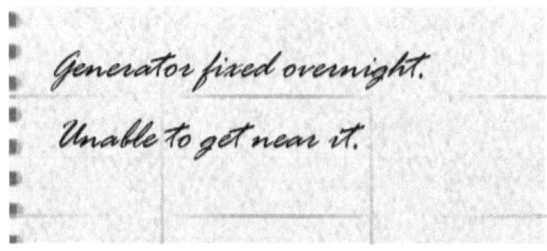

Generator fixed overnight.

Unable to get near it.

After reading it, Vivian tore it into small pieces and flushed it down the toilet.

She considered Rick's note as she ate her breakfast, and decided that she'd go ahead and take the risk. Later that morning, as scheduled, she presented herself at the hospital and went through the same steps as the previous day. Once again, Lisa provided a running commentary as she entered and checked all the computer settings:

```
PATIENT NAME: RULE, VIVIAN
DATE: 82-AUG-06 TIME: 09:45
OPR ID: LISA


TREATMENT MODE: ELECTRON        BEAM ENERGY (MeV):10


                              ACTUAL PRESCRIBED
GANTRY ROTATION (DEG):          45.0     45.0      OK
COLLIMATOR ROTATION (DEG):     359.2    359        OK
COLLIMATOR X (CM):              14.2     14.0      OK
COLLIMATOR Y (CM):              27.1     27.0      OK
WEDGE NUMBER:                       1      1       OK
ACCESSORY NUMBER:                   2      2       OK
```

"OK. Everything looks good." The next line on Lisa's display read:

```
SYSTEM: BEAM READY      OP. MODE: TREAT      AUTO
```

"Stay still now. I'm going to begin." Lisa hit the one-key

command B, for beam on, to begin the treatment. The machine switched on, and Vivian head a low, metallic buzzing that lasted for a full minute.

On her display, Lisa read the computer's summary:

```
TREATMENT MODE: E ENERGY        BEAM ENERGY (MeV):10

                          ACTUAL PRESCRIBED
UNIT RATE/Minute:           200      200
MONITOR UNITS:              200      200
TIME (MIN):                1.01     1.0
```

"Perfect," she said to Vivian over the intercom. "Everything looks good. I'll be right there to help you up."

"Is that it?" asked Vivian, as Lisa approached.

"That's it. How do you feel?"

"I feel fine. In fact, I didn't feel anything at all."

"That's good. Some patients feel like the treatment area gets warm, but your dose wasn't large enough for that. The computer's happy though, and Dr. Wildersbach will be happy too. I'll take him a printout of the results, and he'll see you later about next steps."

Thanking her, Vivian left the hospital, walked over to the dining room to get some tea, and then took it with her to drink down by the marina. As she approached the dock, she spotted Dexter sitting on a wide bench, staring vacantly out over the water.

"It's nice to see you outside and not buried under stacks of computer printouts," she said, when she was close enough.

Startled, he gathered his wits and looked up at her. "Oh, hi. Yes. I'm sitting here, well, because I don't actually know what to do next."

"You mean you've solved the problem?" she asked, sitting down beside him.

"Not solved, no. But I know what it is."

"Would you like to tell me about it?" she prodded. "I probably won't understand anything you say but sometimes when you have to explain a problem to someone else it helps you rethink it."

He blinked, considering. "That's pretty smart. Yes, alright, thank you. Let's try it. I found two problems, actually. The first is in the program itself. Remember what I told you I was doing yesterday?"

Vivian nodded.

"OK. Well, I was on the right track. If an operator needs to make changes the programmers specified a certain way to do it, and they assumed that the operators would follow their instructions. Lisa, on the other hand has used the machine so often that she's learned shortcuts so she can quickly fix typing mistakes. But depending on the mistakes, and the actual keystrokes she uses, it can throw off the assumptions the programmers made about allowing time for the machine motions to happen, so after the mistakes are corrected the display will show that everything is OK, and the program will act like everything's OK, but it might not be OK. Does that make sense so far?"

"I think so, yes. You mentioned yesterday that if something like that happened, the machine might deliver too little radiation, or deliver it over too small or too large and area where it was focused."

"Yes, and I was right.... But you were right too."

"Me?"

"Yes. You asked whether it could lead to overdosing, and it can. In fact, using Lisa's method to correct a single mis-typed setting could lead to the machine delivering a radiation dose that's a hundred times too high. So, if the prescription was for a 200 rad dose over an area of one square centimetre, then the machine could actually deliver a dose of 20,000 rads[46]. Depending on where it was aimed, I think that kind of dosage could seriously injure or kill someone, don't you?"

"I don't know anything about science or medicine, Dexter, but from what you say, I wouldn't be at all surprised.... Didn't you say there were two problems?"

"Yes, it was Lisa who told me about the other one, although she doesn't think of it as a problem. She said that this is the very first of a series of new machines that aren't even on the market yet, and that one of the big features of this machine is that so many of actions are now automatic, including all of the safety features. She said the idea is that having the computer control almost everything is supposed to prevent human errors and therefore eliminate mistakes in the treatment."

"That sounds good."

"It does, but look, I'm taking computer courses at Stanford and spending as much time as I can in their AI Lab[47]. It's probably because I spent so much time working on PDP-10 computers that I got this job, the PDP-11 they have isn't much different from what I'm used to. Anyway, what I was taught was that if you try to automate machines that can cause real harm or damage, then you need to build-in mechanical safeguards so that if the program accidentally tells the machine to do something really stupid, then the mechanical safeguards prevent it. OK?"

"Yes, that seems sensible to me."

"Right. Anyway, according to Lisa, with this machine the developers took out all the mechanical safeguards. I guess they figured that since they'd built lots of safeguards into the program, there was no longer a need to duplicate them with mechanical ones."

"So," Vivian said, thoughtfully, "everything leads back to the program. Can you fix it?"

"Fix it!? No. Well, maybe, I suppose. But it would take, like, forever."

"Have you told the doctor?"

"No. That's why I'm out here thinking. You see, I'm afraid to tell him what I've learned."

Vivian gave him a close look. "Let me guess. You're afraid that there have been accidents in which people have been badly hurt, or worse, but the fact that they've insisted that the mistaken doses were too low to be harmful means that they're trying to hide the fact."

He nodded, looking miserable.

"And that if they find out you've discovered their little secret, they might not be willing to risk allowing you to go home and tell people about it."

He nodded looking a shade paler and, if possible, even more miserable. "It's worse than that, he whispered. "I've actually changed the program and I'm afraid they'll find out."

"What do you mean?"

His words came out in a rush now. "With the generator fixed, I knew you'd be going back for treatment this morning. I was afraid. I mean, what if there was a mistake today and the machine malfunctioned in the bad way. It could have hurt you, or killed you even! When they came and told me last night that the generator had been fixed, so I could go back to working on the program, I couldn't do it, but then I couldn't sleep. So, I got up and went back to the hospital late last night. No one worries about that – I do it all the time – they just think I'm weird and ignore me. Anyway, I added a few lines to the program so no matter what prescription gets entered the machine only puts out a very low dose. Not enough to hurt anyone, but so the machine still makes all the same noises people like Lisa and the doctor are used to hearing."

"You did all that for me?" said Vivian, startled.

"Yes you, and any other patients of course, but mainly because I couldn't stand the thought of you getting hurt when I could have done something about it. So…."

"So you did something about it. Good for you! And, thank you," she said, putting a hand on his arm. "I appreciate what you did.

"You know," she continued thoughtfully, "you look so much like the stereotypical computer nerd that I bet people assume that you're very naïve. But you're not naïve at all are you?"

He smiled weakly. "I know that I'm very introverted and awkward around most people – except you for some reason – maybe that's because you remind me so much of a favourite aunt I have. Anyway, I do pay attention to people, and I've seen things growing up that taught me that people aren't always what they seem, including not being as good as they seem."

"Hmmm. How are you at lying?"

"What?" he said, startled.

"Lying. Can you do it convincingly? Would you be able, for example to keep burying your head in your computer printouts for another day or two, pretend that you're still making progress, and that you think it's just going to be a case of adding a few commands to the program so it does a better job of checking that the machine settings really do match what Lisa enters on the keyboard? And NOT let on what else you've learned?"

He thought about it for a moment. "Yes, I think I could do that," he said. "But what good would that do? After the day or two goes by, they'll expect some kind of results."

She gave him a direct look. "Do you trust me?"

He paused for a moment, considering, then gave a definitive-sounding "Yes."

"OK then. Just keep on with what you've been doing and if anyone asks, make it sound like you're making progress and are optimistic about fixing everything soon and don't let on that you suspect the system of being able to hurt people."

"All right. Ummm. It was you that said I'm not naïve, and no offense intended, but if you think you can help me you must be something more than just an ordinary, but nice, widow."

She gave him a brilliant smile, lowered her voice for effect, and said "I am indeed, and I promise to tell you all about it later."

7 CALL TO ACTION

Leaving Dexter on the bench, Vivian walked up the hill and made for the dining room. It was not yet lunchtime so there were only two men having coffee in one corner of the hall. They looked like guides.

Vivian walked over to the serving window and, in a voice that was just loud enough for the men to hear, said "Rick, could I make a special request for dinner tonight?"

"Probably," said Rick, as he approached the window.

When he got there, Vivian made sure her back was turned towards the two men and leaned in towards Rick. In a much lower voice, she related what Dexter had just admitted and her concern that he was not likely to be a good enough actor to fool the doctor if questioned.

"I think we'll need to have him extracted," she concluded.

Rick nodded, thinking quickly. "Do you know about the little suburb of houses near the point?"

She nodded. "Yes. The doctor and I walked over there last night. That's probably as good a pickup point as any."

"I'll go try to get Alex and Don on the radio and arrange it for just before twilight. If anyone hears a boat near there, they'll assume it's one of the Northern Angler's boats heading back to their camp."

With a curt nod, Vivian turned away and, in a louder voice, said "Thanks Rick. See you later."

"No problem, I just have to dig out a few supplies."

As Vivian walked out the front door and headed for her house, Rick walked out the back door, heading for his. On his way, he was careful to make sure he wasn't being followed and that his house wasn't under surveillance, then went in and retrieved the police radio from its hiding place in the attic. Turning it on, he said "Cat calling. Cat calling." After waiting twenty seconds or so, he repeated the call.

There was a lengthy pause, and Rick was just about to try again when the radio crackled.

***

"Dog here, go ahead Cat," I replied from the houseboat, having heard his call and gone inside.

The code words were really just a means of making sure no one had stolen one of the radios. With the proper words having been spoken, Rick switched to plain English, relying on the radios' encryption for security.

"We need an extraction. There's a computer whiz kid here that helped us, and now Vivian thinks he's in danger of being found out. Can you pick him up at the little collection of houses located near the west end of the peninsula? They should be marked on one of the site drawings Don has."

"Wait one," I said, which was a shorthand way of saying 'Wait just a moment.'

Don had come inside in time to hear Rick's request and was reaching for a file of documents. Flipping through it, he pulled out a surface plan of the site as it had been in 1957.

"Got it. What time?"

"Uncertain, but assume just before twilight. Can you bring a handheld, in case things change?"

We knew that every moment Rick was on his radio increased the chances of being discovered, so I simply replied, "Will do. Out."

"His name is Dexter. Out."

"We'll have to take the inflatable," said Don. "If we all go, I can stay with the boat and keep watch while you and Silver get the kid. Silver should be able to help find him and sniff out any threats."

"I agree. We'll need to pack a few things."

***

When Vivian walked into the dining hall an hour later, it was just beginning to fill up. She noticed that Dexter was sitting by himself at a table surrounded by piles of computer printouts, as usual. This time, she ignored him completely and simply went to the serving window to select her lunch. As she was ladling soup into a bowl, she happened to glance up and see Rick standing to one side in the kitchen, watching her. When their eyes met, he gave a slight nod and tapped the side of his nose with his right index figure. Without giving any indication she'd even seen him she took up her lunch tray and went to sit at an empty table some distance away from everyone else. If Dexter even saw her come in, he gave no sign of it.

When she had finished her lunch, she took her tray to the clean-up area, dropped it off and walked to the door. As she did so, Dexter raised his head, spotted her and gave her a hopeful look. She didn't say anything, but as she passed by, she looked him straight in the eye and casually winked, then continued on out the door.

That's all I can do for him right now, she thought. *We'll have to see what happens next.*

In fact, nothing much happened for the next several hours, until late in the afternoon when Dr. Ernst Wildersbach entered the dining hall and walked over to Dexter's table.

"Still at it, I see," he said.

"Yes sir," replied Dexter, looking up at him and pushing the bridge of his glasses up on his nose. "I think I've found the problem and I'm just working out the changes I'll need to make. There are quite a few lines of code that will have to be changed." For illustration, he held up a sheet of computer printout on which several lines of code had been circled, with new lines hand-printed in the margin beside them.

None of this was comprehensible to the doctor, but he would never have admitted that. Instead, he went on offence. "Well hurry it up, can't you? It's taking too long. Why, if I didn't know better, I'd suspect you were just wasting time while you rest here using up my accommodations and my food and money!"

"N-n-no sir," stammered Dexter, who had turned white and recoiled. "I would never do that."

"Well, see that you get it fixed. I want it finished tomorrow, even if you have to stay up all night, understand?"

"Y-y-yes sir," replied Dexter as the doctor stormed out.

A short time later, Vivian returned to the dining hall hoping to have a quiet chat with Rick. The lunch patrons were long gone with the sole exception of Dexter, who was sitting in his usual place. The only difference was that, although he was surrounded by the usual pile of printouts and hand-written notes, he wasn't working on them but was simply sitting there looking dejected.

"What's the matter Dexter?" she asked. "You look pale and troubled."

He looked around to make sure they were alone, the replied "The doctor was just here chewing me out for not being finished yet. Then he yelled at me and said that I had to be finished by tomorrow, even if I had to work all night."

"So why not just tell him you're finished. It will take them some time to discover what you've done."

"I could say the words, but I don't think I can fool him. When he was here just now, I tried lying about my progress, but I could feel myself turning pale and I kind of seized-up and started stammering like I used to do when I was younger. I think he might have interpreted it as me being intimidated by him, which I am, but I think he'll catch on if I try to keep it up."

Vivian looked at him consideringly, then came to a decision. "Yes, you're probably right at that.... Still trust me?"

"Yes," he said immediately.

"OK then. Is all this," she pointed at the table, "the whole program and all of your notes?"

"Yes. Everything."

"And is there anything back where you're staying that you absolutely can't live without?"

He considered it. "Just my passport, I guess."

"OK. Pile all this up in some kind of order, then leave it here and go get your passport and come straight back here. Got it?"

"OK. If you say so."

"I do. And Dexter, just walk casually, don't rush. Imagine you're just taking your time strolling there and back as if you don't have a care in the world, and for heaven's sake don't furtively look around to see if anyone's watching. Just act oblivious to everything. OK?"

"OK. Whatever you say."

"Good. Do it now. I'll be here waiting for you."

After Dexter had finished sorting out the paper, he left the dining room as instructed. Vivian then went to the serving window to find that Rick had been standing right there on the other side, but to one side where he would be hidden from the sight and anyone not standing close by.

"Trouble?" he said.

Vivian nodded. "The doctor's getting cranky and Dexter's rattled. I think we need to get him out now. He'll be a perfect witness if any of this ever goes to trial and I don't want him disappearing on us."

Rick nodded. "I got through to Alex and Don. They'll be at the point just before twilight. Around 9:30 or 10 pm, say."

"That's a long time to wait but it will have to do. Is there a way he can get there through the woods, so no one will see him?"

"Yes. I'll take him so he doesn't get lost and I'll find a nice house to break into so he can hide. I can make sure we're not followed, too. Is he going to need all that stuff?" he asked, looking at the piles of paper on the table Dexter had vacated.

"Yes. He has the whole computer program printed out and he knows why it doesn't always work, and he knows it's capable of injuring or killing the patients."

Rick gave a low whistle. "No wonder you want to spirit him away. We've got them."

"Almost. We still don't know what happened to your colleague or the senator."

"No, but we have a pretty good idea. Anyway, it turns out that the camp's 'Lost and Found' department is right here in the kitchen. If you grab his stuff, I'll liberate a backpack."

By the time Dexter returned, Vivian had stuffed his papers into a backpack while Rick had filled the rest of the space with bottles of water and pre-made, bagged sandwiches from one of the kitchen's fridges. Vivian waved Dexter over and made introductions.

"Rick, this is Dexter. Dexter, this is Rick. You can trust him. He's going to take you to a house way out at the point and you're to stay hidden until this evening when someone will come for you. Can you do that?"

"I think so," he said. "How will I recognize them and how will they know where I'll be hiding?"

"They won't know, at first, but it will be a woman with red hair and a dog that looks like a wolf. The woman's a Mountie, and the dog's a police dog. The dog will find you."

"A real Mountie?" he asked, "like in the movies?"

"No Mountie is like the Hollywood versions, although now that you mention it, this one actually comes pretty close, and she's real all right. Stick with them and they'll keep you safe. OK?"

Dexter looked at her, then at Rick, then pushed his glasses up on the bridge of his nose. "Who are you people anyway?"

"For now, just think of us as two people that are helping you. The woman's name is Alex. She'll answer all your questions once she gets you away from here. Rick and I will catch up with you in a day or two." She looked at Rick. "All set?"

"All set," he replied. "Dexter, all your papers are in here, plus some food and water." He handed it over so Dexter could put it on. To Vivian, he said "If you need it, I hid my camera bag in the attic of my house."

"Right. Thanks. Dexter: go with Rick and do what he says."

"OK Mrs. Rule. Thank you."

"Come in through here Dexter," said Rick, opening a door that was located beside the broad serving window. "We're going out the back way." To Vivian, he said, "I'll see you at supper."

Rick led Dexter to the back door of the dining hall, then said "We'll split up for the first part so if anyone spots either of us they won't think anything of it. I want you to walk down the road to the hospital, just like you do all the time. If anyone challenges you, you're on your way to the hospital to continue with your programming. If they search your pack, the food is in case you need to work late on the program just like the doctor told you to do.

"Next. When you get to the hospital, walk right past it, turn right and follow the road to the small lake that's back there. I'll meet you there."

"OK."

"Good. Off you go then."

As Dexter walked the familiar route to the hospital, Rick let him get almost out of sight before setting out himself on a route that took him past the buildings that were being used as dormitories and even the ones behind them that weren't in use at all, as evidenced by the profusion of broken windows. As he passed the latter buildings, he increased his walking pace and made a sharp turn around the last building so he could peek back to see if anyone was following. When he was satisfied, and moving quickly then, he entered the nearby woods and followed a series of game trails that took him past the rear of the hospital. As he neared Blair Lake, he was relieved to see Dexter walking towards him. Being well hidden in the trees, he startled Dexter by calling out to him when he was only a few feet away.

"Phew. You scared me there for a moment," said Dexter. "I didn't see you at all."

"Sorry. Come crouch down beside me here for a moment. I want to see if you're being followed."

Dexter did so and tried to emulate Rick, who was intently scanning the buildings and roads that were within their view. After a while, he became restless and began to fidget.

"Stay still," Rick admonished. "One of the so-called guides is crafty and knows how to shadow a person. If he's following you, he isn't dumb enough to be obvious about it."

Wrapping his arms around his chest, Dexter hugged himself tightly and focused on holding still.

After what seemed like forever, Rick looked over at him, smiled, and said "Good job. Staying still and remaining vigilant doesn't come naturally to most people. It's a skill. I think the coast is clear. Let's get moving." With Rick in the lead, the two men walked roughly northwest, following an obviously much-used game trail that ran alongside the lakeshore. After about a quarter of a mile (400 m) however, Rick changed course to southwest, saying "From here we cut through the forest until we come to a kind of suburb of small, abandoned houses." Although their destination was only about 1,500 feet (450 m) 'as the crow flies,' they had to walk at least three or four times that distance by following game trails. Just when Dexter was beginning to feel like they'd never get out of the forest, he almost tripped over something. It was a white picket fence, or at least it had been at one time, and it surrounded a little house and backyard, with the remnants of a children's swing set and a scattering of old, rusting metal toys.

"We've arrived," said Rick. "Let's head for the houses that are closest to the point." Moving around the house, they followed the old road in a counter-clockwise direction until they found themselves at a house that actually looked out from the point with an almost panoramic view of the big lake.

As Dexter watched, Rick went all the way around the house, testing windows and doors as he went. When he arrived at the back, he found the door was unlocked so he walked in. A quick check of the rooms showed that the house hadn't been used in a very long time.

"This should be as good a place as any to hide out," he said to Dexter. "You've got food and water, so all you have to do is lie low and wait for evening. You'll hear a small boat of some kind approach. They'll have to find a place to beach, so it might not be right in front of you but it shouldn't be far away. You're looking for a woman with red hair and a dog."

"What if they don't come?" asked Dexter, in a worried voice.

"If they don't make it, stay here and stay quiet. Either Vivian or I will come back, but it will be very late at night. OK?"

"OK."

"I have to leave you now so I can get back and get everything ready for tonight's supper."

"What are you? You can't be just a cook."

"For now, let's just say that I also cook. I promise to tell you more in a few days," and with that, Rick left.

When suppertime arrived, Vivian walked into the dining hall and immediately went to get a tray and get her food.

"How are things with you?" she asked, when Rick came to the serving window to explain the evening's meal options.

"Just fine, thank you" he said. "Just another day in the great Canadian north."

Satisfied, she made her meal choices and went to a table. Once again, she was joined mid-meal by the doctor.

"How are you feeling after your first treatments, my dear?" he asked.

"Fine, I think. I don't actually feel any different at all."

"No. No, that's as it should be. The dosages we used were low. We'll do another set every day for the next four days, then give you two days of rest, and then we'll reassess where we are."

"Did you have a busy day besides treating me?"

"Yes. Yes. In fact, we have two other patients beginning treatment. One of them is going to be a difficult case. Quite urgent, really, and we're going to have to use very high energy treatments, but let's not dwell on my problems."

Vivian allowed him to deftly shift their conversation to other topics.

Saturday, August 7

Vivian's next treatment had been scheduled for 10:30 am in the morning. Her guess that they'd had another patient in before her was confirmed by the fact that the doctor and Lisa were discussing it when she walked in.

"And he didn't notice anything, you say. Nothing at all?" Dr. Wildersbach was saying.

"No doctor. I asked him more than once," Lisa replied.

"That can't be right. We need to hit that spot hard and at the intensity and duration I prescribed he should have felt the area heat up. The machine must have...." he broke off, having seen Vivian walk in. "Where is that infernal kid anyway? If he's changed the program without my approval, I'll skin him alive!"

"He hasn't been in yet today doctor. Normally he's already in here working before I arrive but there was no one here this morning. I thought he might not be feeling well, so I asked one of the guides to go check on him. When he came back, he said that Dexter wasn't in his room and that he hadn't shown up for breakfast either."

"That's odd. Very odd. And this is a fine time for him to disappear, just when we're in the middle of...." He glanced at Vivian again and didn't finish the sentence, but his anger was clearly rising.

Taking a step towards Vivian, he caught her arm with one hand, saying "Vivian. You were talking to him yesterday. How did he seem to you?"

"Well, he was buried in all those printouts and notes like usual, and he's not really a people person, so we just exchanged a few pleasantries, but he seemed distracted to me."

Dr. Wildersbach reddened, tightened his grip and shook her

arm. "You were talking to him for more than just a minute. It must have been more than a few pleasantries. What else did he say?"

"Ernst! You're hurting me! I don't even remember what we talked about. I was just trying to be nice and draw him out a bit, but it didn't work. He said that all he's been doing here is checking the computer program for you and he hasn't time to do anything else, no fishing, no anything else really."

With an effort, the doctor took a deep breath, regained control of himself, and released his grip on Vivian's arm. "Apologies. My apologies. I shouldn't have gotten excited and taken it out on you. I've been under a lot of stress lately and didn't sleep well last night, but that's no reason to take it out on you. I apologise."

"It's OK Ernst, I understand."

In a calmer voice, he said "Did you see him at any other time yesterday?"

"I don't think... wait a minute. Yes I did. It was later in the afternoon. I saw him walking down the main road. You know, towards all those mine buildings and that big, tall scaffold-like tower."

"The headframe, you mean."

"Yes, I guess that's what you call it. I don't mean that he was necessarily going to it, only that he was walking in that direction." Vivian paused, then continued. "You don't think he would have gone exploring inside those buildings, do you? They look dangerous to me, with those roofs looking like they are about to collapse and who knows what machinery and chemicals falling apart inside."

"Hmmm. Hmmm. Maybe you're right. Those buildings are too dangerous to enter, but he's young enough to have done something stupid like that. I suppose I'll have to get some of the guides to go search for him." Muttering to himself, he stalked out of the hospital.

"Does he get angry and flare-up like that often?" Vivian asked Lisa.

"Oh no, not the doctor," said Lisa, but her eyes and facial expression said something entirely different. She seemed to be struggling with something for a moment, then she leaned closer and lowered her voice. "I shouldn't be telling you this, but we lost a patient this morning. I think that's why he's so upset."

"That makes it easier to understand. Thank you for telling me."

While Lisa went ahead with her treatment, Vivian was feeling very relaxed and composed with this second one, knowing that Dexter had changed the computer program to ensure she only received a safe dosage. When it was over and Vivian left the hospital, she tried to walk like she was just out for a casual stroll, but her destination was the dining hall. The dining room was empty when she got there, and she found that Rick was in the kitchen with the beginnings of lunch preparations.

"Things are heating up," she said. "They had a patient die this morning, which seems to have put the doctor in a foul mood. On top of that, he's become suspicious that Dexter might have altered the computer program and he's now organizing some of the guides to search for him."

"Good thing we got Dexter out last night then. I think I'll take a fresh mug of coffee over to my friend Alistair in the hospital. I might be able to find out whether the body is still there. If it is, I'd like to know what they ultimately do with it."

"Me too," she agreed.

That same day (Saturday, August 7)

It was quiet when Rick entered the hospital with his trademark mug of special coffee for Alistair. He was only putting a third of a pill in each mug now, to ensure that Alistair was continuing to show 'improvement' without yet feeling quite well. In fact, when Rick asked him about his recovery, he said that he was doing better eating more, and holding it down. "I think another day or two and I'll be able to return to the kitchen. That will put you out of a job I'm afraid."

"That's OK," laughed Rick. "I enjoyed it, and I still got lots of fishing in, but it's about time I went back home."

"I'm going to miss your special coffees."

"Well, you're very welcome. At least as chief cook you know how to make your own when the need arises…. By the way," he added, as if it has just occurred to him. "I heard a rumour that a patient died this morning."

"We're not supposed to know about that kind of thing," replied Alistair, "but yes, and it's been happening about once a month. The patient that died is in the next room." He indicated the direction with a tip of his head.

"Really, one a month. What do they do with the bodies, ship them home?"

"No. It's odd but they don't ship them out and no family members ever come to collect them." He waved Rick closer to his bed and lowered his voice to a whisper. "I don't think they even tell the relatives, or anyone else, when a patient dies."

"Really? Why? And what do they do with the bodies then?"

"I don't know the answer to either. I've heard the guides complaining sometimes though, when the doctor and Delorme aren't around. They get told to carry the bodies off and dump them somewhere, but I don't know where."

"Stranger and stranger," said Rick. "You think they just dump them in the lake?"

"Could be. It's deep enough if you go out a ways and from the complaints I heard it seems like they only take them out at night when it's dark."

"Sounds like a plot for a horror movie. Evil doctor conducts gruesome experiments and the bodies are dumped in the lake."

"I don't know, and I don't want to know. And you heard nothing from me, right?"

"Right," said Rick. "Well, I have to get back and make sure I'm ready for the lunch crowd. Enjoy your coffee."

Alistair raised his mug in salute as Rick left.

Meanwhile the previous day (Friday, August 6)

It was a relief to receive the radio call from Rick since it had been over three days since I'd seen Vivian and over six since Rick had flown to the fishing camps, and we readily agreed to extract the 'whiz kid.' There wasn't a lot to plan or prepare, so we mostly just had to wait, Don's joke about us having to 'standby to standby[48]' had worn thin, and I'd become impatient.

When it was time to go, we all got into the inflatable boat and Don piloted us to the pickup site. This involved motoring among the many small islands that lie off the southwest point of the peninsula. When we emerged from between the islands, Don headed along St. Mary's Channel as if we were just another motorboat heading for the Northern Angler fishing camp, which would take us around the Crackingstone Point and into Black Bay.

Of course, we were headed for the point itself and, at the last minute, Don turned us to starboard, and we began looking for a safe place to land.

Having beached the inflatable, and tied it to a sturdy-looking tree, Don selected a position from which he could keep watch and guard the boat, while Silver and I made for the small community of houses near the point that was shown on the Gunner Mining Limited's drawings we'd reviewed.

I didn't have to give any special command to Silver. The mere fact that I was creeping along stealthily and looking around told him all he needed to know. As we approached the houses, I was just trying to decide how to go about our search when Silver's ears perked up and he began staring at the house that was nearest the point.

"Is there someone there, Silver? Let's go see." With Silver at my side, I walked up to the front door and knocked. Glancing down at Silver, I could see that he didn't look concerned - he obviously wasn't sensing danger at the moment – so I simply knocked on the door and called out "Dexter? Police."

There was a scuffing sound and a young man's voice said "This door's jammed somehow, but the back door is open."

"OK," I said, "we'll meet you there." When we reached the back door there was a young man waiting for us. He was wearing a backpack, and he looked and sounded scared.

"You're Dexter, I presume?" He nodded. "Hi. I'm Sergeant Alex Houston, RCMP, and this is my partner, Silver." I took out my wallet and showed him my badge. "We're working undercover. That's why we're not in uniform. Are you ready to get out of here?"

"You bet I am," he said.

"OK. Stay close behind me. We're not going to move quickly, partly so no one trips in this low light and partly because I want Silver to be able to hear or smell the approach of anyone that might be unfriendly. When we get to the shore, we'll be met by a rather large man, but it's OK, he's with us. Come on."

Although I was being cautious, our short walk back to where we'd tied up the boat was uneventful, except that Dexter nearly jumped out of his skin when Don suddenly, and quietly, materialized out of the gloom from where he'd been watching.

"Sorry about that," I said. "Silver didn't react because he knows

Don's scent. This is Don. Don, this is Dexter. We can all get better acquainted when we're away from here."

"Right. Hi Dexter, pleased to meet you," said Don. "Let's push the boat out a bit so you three can hop in."

In a few moments we had untied the boat, pushed it off the beach, and Dexter, Silver, and I had climbed in. After giving it a last push-off with his legs, Don scrambled in as well, and made his way back to the motor, started it, and put it in reverse so we could back away. When we were clear, Don headed us back into the channel, from which we retraced out route back to the houseboat.

When we reached the houseboat, Dexter asked Don whether he was a Mountie too.

"No, he said, I'm just another part of the team," and so saying, he produced his military police ID and badge. "What's in the backpack?" he asked, changing the subject, "it looks full."

Dexter explained what he'd been doing at the camp, ending with the fact that he had a complete printout of the computer program plus his notes on the bugs in the program and how they could affect the machine settings.

"There you go," I said, "some kind of intermittent machine malfunction was one of the things we'd speculated on. It was Rick's thought that it might be caused by problems in the computer program."

"Why was Vivian so insistent that I bring everything with me?"

"Well, probably because it's the way she thinks. She's a Special Agent with the FBI, and she's thinking ahead to a potential court case."

"Wow, FBI too, plus RCMP and military police. What's Rick then?"

Don and I looked at each other for a moment. "What did he tell you?"

"He admitted that he's more than just a cook, but didn't explain what he meant. He only said that he'd tell me more in a couple of days."

"Hmmm. We should leave it at that for now. He is working undercover and with us, though, as you've already figured out."

We spent the next hour or so getting as much information as we could about the camp, the various people in it and, of course, Rick and Vivian.

"Know anything about a guide called Delorme?" asked Don at

one point.

Dexter nodded. "Not much, but I used to visit my uncle's ranch a lot back home. If this was a ranch, then I guess Delorme would be the foreman, because he's the one that gives everybody orders, and he's the one that the other guides complain about when he isn't around. One of them claims Delorme was a mercenary fighting in South Africa before he came here."

"Hmmm," said Don, "that certainly matches my first impression of him: ex-military."

From everything Dexter had told us, it seemed unlikely that his disappearance would be discovered until the next day, but to play safe, Don and I decided to alternate watches overnight. We knew that we could count on Silver to alert us to anyone's approach, but we thought it best to have at least one person that was more or less fully awake in case prompt action was required. Dexter was amused to see us flip a coin to determine the watches. I drew the first watch (20:00 to midnight), Don the middle watch (midnight to 04:00) and then me again for the morning watch (04:00 to 08:00). That also meant Don had to cook our breakfast in the morning.

Dexter's amusement was short-lived however, and he sobered up instantly when he saw us dig out our travelling gun cases, unlock them, and load our pistols. Although Don settled and fell asleep almost immediately, the sounds of constant tossing and turning suggested that Dexter was having trouble settling. After about an hour, I noticed that Dexter had quieted down and that Silver wasn't beside me anymore. Curious, I got up and crept quietly inside the houseboat and along to peek in the open door of the small cabin we'd made available for him.

"Hi," said Dexter, when he saw me.

"Everything OK?" I asked.

"It is now. I was worrying about everything, especially Vivian back there at the camp, and Silver must have sensed it because he came in here, jumped up on the bunk, and stretched himself out right beside me. That was cool, and it was comforting having him lay here with me, but the interesting thing was when I noticed him staring at me."

"Oh?"

"Yeah. You're going to think I'm crazy, but as I looked into his eyes, it was like he was trying to tell me to relax – that everything was going to be OK."

I smiled. "Well, if you're crazy then I am too, because he does that kind of thing to me all the time. I don't understand it, but I love it.... Good boy Silver!"

Leaving the two of them, I went back to my watching position up on the roof of the houseboat. It wasn't long before I heard Silver scrambling up the steps and felt him nestle in beside me.

"How's Dexter doing?" I asked him, not expecting a response, but the sounds of snoring coming from down below gave me my answer anyway.

"Well done, Silver," I congratulated, giving him an ear rub.

It was a beautiful night, although at this latitude[49] (59°23' N) and this time of year, there was no true nighttime. Nautical twilight[50] began around 22:20 and astronomical twilight was just setting in – and my ability to make out the horizon was fast disappearing - when Don relieved me at midnight. It was back to nautical twilight when I relieved Don at 04:00. The sky had changed from a dim, bluish-cast to distinctly light, and I could see the horizon and make out shapes on our boat and the nearby shore. Although I was sleepy, it was actually quite a beautiful time to just sit out and feel alone in the world while watching the sun rise up above the horizon.

8 CONVERGENCE

Saturday, August 7

As it turned out, our caution had been unnecessary that night. I didn't hear any boats come remotely near us. Our morning was similarly uneventful, but all that changed right after lunchtime, when we received a radio call from Rick.

"They had a patient die this morning," he began, "and I've been told that the guides take the bodies away and dispose of them when that happens. If so, I want to know how and where, so I'm planning to follow them if I can. I'm guessing that the quietest times are either mid-afternoon when the customers are out fishing and the patients are being examined or treated, or else late at night."

"Do you want us to come in as backup?" I asked.

"Yes. I'm not confident of my ability to keep eluding Delorme, but I think you should wait for my call."

"Agreed. We'll be ready. Out."

The prospect of providing backup for Rick, and possibly Vivian as well, forced us to make a decision on whether one of us should remain behind to guard Dexter. In the end, we decided that we should put Dexter into hiding on the island to which the houseboat was moored. With this in mind, we filled his backpack with some essentials including several flares, so that, if something happened to us, he could attempt to signal a passing boat or the regular supply barge from Fond du Lac. We also gave him one of the handheld police radios with instructions to listen-in only, and not try to call out except in case of emergency. I wrote out a list of our agreed-upon code names, then added one for him: 'Turtle.'

"Turtle?" he asked, sounding a bit offended.

"Well," I said, "there's no point in giving you a code-name like 'Hacker' or Whiz-Kid,' is there?"

"Ah. Good point," he said, sounding mollified and even a bit pleased.

It turned out to be a good thing that we made our preparations for Dexter promptly. Don and I both expected that we'd be waiting until late at night, but it was only about an hour later that we received another call from Rick.

"They're on the move," he reported. "A truck just pulled up to the rear of the hospital and two of the guides loaded what could have been a body, wrapped in a sheet, into the back. I'm in the woods behind the hospital.... Wait one."

There was a minute or two of silence, then: "OK. They're heading east, so probably towards the old dock, the flooded pit, the waste rock piles, or the tailings area. I'm going to follow them. I'll collect Vivian on the way if I can. My next messages may be very short in order to minimize the chances of being overheard."

"Roger that. We'll head for the shipping dock. Out," I replied.

***

When the guides had driven away with the large bundle in the back of their truck, Rick emerged from hiding and walked directly to Vivian's house and gave her the latest news. She decided to join him and the two of them were walking toward the dining hall when they noticed a truck parked by one of the nearby dormitory buildings.

"What do you think?" asked Vivian.

"In a remote place like this, I bet they just leave the keys in the vehicles. There's no risk of theft here."

Rick was right. When they reached the truck, the keys were in the ignition, so they simply climbed in and drove off in the direction Rick had seen the guides go.

***

Leaving Dexter on the little island as planned, Don, Silver, and I had taken the inflatable boat and headed straight for the shipping dock. As soon as we got out of the boat and had a chance to look around, we noticed a pickup truck parked by the one of the old buildings that had been cleaned-up and converted to storage. While Don went to have a look at the truck, Silver and I went to see what was going on in the storage building.

When we went back and met up with Don, he said "Anything happening in there?"

"Sort of," I replied. "One of the staff is just inside the door taking a nap."

"That's a help," Don chuckled. "We're in luck here too, the keys are still in the ignition." Opening the door, he got in and waited while Silver and I went to the other side and climbed in as well.

As we drove off, my portable radio crackled to life.

"Mouse calling. Mouse calling." It was Vivian.

"Dog here. Go ahead Mouse."

"We've borrowed a truck – black in colour - and are trying to catch up to the two guides. They are in a red truck."

"We've borrowed a truck as well. It's white. We are currently positioned by the headframe."

Suddenly Rick chimed in: "We have their dust in sight ahead of us, Dog. Wait one."

There was a pause while Rick attempted to close the distance and see which way the guide's truck would turn. "They're veering north around the pit," reported Vivian.

"Roger that. We see them crossing our line of sight as well," I confirmed. "We'll move around the southern side of the pit and hold."

Don drove along the narrow path that was all that was left of a former service road that ran between the mine's open pit and the huge waste rock pile.

After only a few minutes, Vivian came back on the radio. "They've passed the turn-off to the tailings... now they're passing the acid plants... now turning south. They're either heading for the east side of the pit or the waste rock pile."

I gave a double click on my radio to confirm that we'd received the message.

"My money's on the pit," said Don. "I bet that's why the rowboat is tied up there."

"I think you're right," I agreed, as Don started the truck and moved us a bit closer to the east side of the pit.

***

Unbeknownst to us, Rick had come to the same prediction as Don and was explaining to Vivian about finding the rowboat tied up at the flooded pit.

"I don't suppose you're armed?" he asked Vivian.

She shook her head. "No."

"Here." Rick passed over a six-inch chef's knife in an improvised sheath that he'd made out of cardboard and duct tape.

"Thanks. What about you?"

"I have a smaller one in my boot, and I also have a few of these." He reached down to his right-side, pant-leg cargo pocket, opened it and extracted a stick of dynamite.

Vivian raised her eyebrows. "Remind me not to mess with you in future. That must be pretty old. Do you think it's stable?"

"I doubt it. These sticks are called forcite, which used to be common in the mining industry. I know it's supposed to be waterproof, so that helps, but I don't think it will take much to set them off. Anyway, these are the only weapons we have, so they'll have to do."

After a few more minutes, Vivian got back on the radio. "They've turned. We're going to hold up until we see whether they take the next turn or not…. OK. They've turned again – Rick says it's the pit for sure.

"You have jurisdiction here. Do you want to move in and have us stay back?"

"Yes please. We're moving now."

***

With Rick and Vivian keeping watch, Don drove around the side of the pit and down the same short road that Rick and Vivian saw the guides take. Sure enough, they were parked exactly where we'd parked when we'd fished there, and Don immediately stopped the truck so we could try to assess what they were doing. I was surprised to realize that had only been the previous day. So much had happened that it seemed further away than that.

We had a fairly clear view, and it appeared that each of the guides was walking along the fringe of the trees, stopping and bending over once in a while as if looking for something. It wasn't long before one of them straightened up from one such exercise, holding something in both hands.

"Rocks," said Don. "You know what those are for."

I was already thumbing the transmit button on my radio. "Bingo. They're collecting rocks. We'll be moving in shortly."

Vivian gave a double-click in response.

We'd no sooner completed this exchange than the other guide had picked something up and was walking toward the first, who was out of our sight behind their truck.

"Let's go," I said, and Don and I opened the doors of our truck, climbed out, along with Silver, and left the doors open rather than risk the sounds associated with closing them. By this time, both guides were out of sight behind their truck. Using only hand gestures and eye movements, Don and I quickly agreed to approach from opposite side of their truck, so he veered to the left and the forest side, while Silver and I veered to the right on the side of the flooded pit.

When I had swung around enough to see the guides again, they were both kneeling down, working on something to do with the large bundle, and completely oblivious to us. I looked across at Don, who nodded, and kept on walking toward the guides. I was just about as close as I wanted to get, and was about to speak, when one of the guides suddenly looked up, saw me, and jumped to his feet.

"Hey! Who are you and what are you doing here?"

"Police!" I called. "Both of you get up and put your hands in the air."

The one that was already standing put his hands up, looking apprehensive, but the other guide snarled something I couldn't make out and drew a large knife from a belt sheath as he stood up.

"I don't think so," he said, beginning to walk towards me and holding the knife in an offensive position. "Why don't you just turn around, missy, and get out of here while you still can?"

Everything he'd just done set off alarm bells in Silver's head, who snarled and immediately moved ahead and to the right of me so he could take up a flanking position in a maneuver the two of us had carried out so many times before, in so many other dangerous situations, that I hadn't had to give him any kind of signal or instruction. What I did do, was take out my snub-nosed .38 Special revolver and point it at the guide, saying "Police! Drop the knife, stand still, and raise your hands. That's your second warning. You won't get a third."

"Everyone knows Canadian police don't shoot first! Why don't you just put that away and leave us alone. Otherwise, I'm going to come over there and take that little pea-shooter away from you."

"I think you've been watching too many movies, friend," said Don's voice from behind the guides. "Trust me. She'll shoot you if you make her."

"Bullshit," the man said and came toward me with is knife up, in a fighting crouch.

"Silver!" I called, and made a motion with my hand.

In almost the same instant Silver exploded toward the guide from the side, like a coiled spring. It was amazing how fast he could accelerate for such a big dog.

His movement caught the guide off guard and he was slow to react. By the time he had turned to face this new threat and decided how he wanted to hold the knife, Silver had advanced close enough to spring and threw himself into the air. The results were that Silver was able to encase the guide's knife hand in his big jaws, his momentum and weight threw the guide off-balance, and the two of them dropped down to the ground – with Silver's jaws firmly attached to the guide's hand which was still holding the knife and, for the moment, incapable of letting it go. By that point, the guide's initial scream of agony had morphed into a series of moans.

While Don came up and handcuffed the first guide, I told Silver to release the second, allowing the knife to drop to the ground while the guide cradled his injured hand. With Don watching the guide, I moved in and picked up the knife. The guides' truck had a small first aid kit, enabling us to dress the second guide's wounded hand and then we handcuffed him as well.

With Don and I each taking a guide by the arm, we walked

them over to the water's edge where the large, sheet-wrapped bundle had been placed in the bow of the rowboat. It was certainly about the right size for an adult body, and was secured by several lengths of rope tied around it at intervals along its length. Tied to two of these ropes were mesh bags that appeared to have been made from sections of fishing net. Inside each bag were the rocks the guides had been seen collecting by the trees.

Before touching anything, I ran back to our borrowed truck, moved it closer to the rowboat, and retrieved the camera that I had brought with me. I used it to capture shots of the bundle in the rowboat from several angles. When that was done, we took a closer look at the boat. There wasn't much doubt about what was in the wrapped bundle, but I took out my knife and cut one of the ropes so I could partially unwrap the sheet at about where I thought the face might be. I'll skip providing a graphic description and just report that it was a human male that had clearly been dead for some hours. After Don had taken a look as well, I re-wrapped the exposed part and secured it with the cut piece of rope.

"I didn't know what was in there," protested the first guide. "We were just following orders."

"Shut up you idiot," snarled the second guide, whose attitude had not been improved by having Silver lacerate his hand.

"We'll take statements from each of you later," I said. "We have a few other things to do first." Standing up, I made a radio call to Vivian and Rick. They would have been watching the action, so all I had to do was tell them about the body, and confirm that the guides were in custody.

"What next?" asked Vivian.

"I think our priority now should be to find the doctor, before he hears about all this and tries to slip away. After that, we can radio the Uranium City RCMP Detachment[51] for help."

Up until that point, all four of us had avoided Uranium City for fear of inadvertently making anyone suspicious of us being anything other than the cover-story images we'd tried to project, but the need for secrecy would most likely be gone once we had the doctor in custody.

Vivian responded with a double click, and I suggested they wait where they were and we would go to them. First though, we loaded the two guides and the wrapped body into the truck's open box. With the two guides in a sitting position, hands manacled behind them, we passed a sturdy-looking rope between their arms and the cargo hooks on each side of the box. This gave them enough slack to shift position but not enough to get up or out of the box. This wasn't the absolute safest position for them to be in, but we didn't want them together in the back seat of our truck either. When we were loaded, I radioed Vivian that we were on our way.

Once we'd met up with Vivian and Rick, we decided to drive to the area where the hospital and dining hall were, to begin searching for the doctor. With Rick and Vivian in the lead, we drove past the acid plants, and their truck was just passing the flooded pit and the turn-off to the headframe and main dock, when a shot rang out and the front-right corner of their truck suddenly sagged.

"Must have taken out the tire," said Rick, struggling to retain control. Fortunately, neither truck had been moving very quickly over the broken and rutted road, so he was able to resume control and immediately threw the truck into reverse and stomped on the gas.

In our truck, Don had braked hard and immediately shifted into reverse when we heard the shot, so we were already backing up when Rick began to do the same.

Meanwhile, right after the first shot, there was another loud crack, then another, and then another. One of these hit the front passenger-side tire of Rick's truck, one missed the truck completely, and the last one struck the windshield and went right through creating a small hole with a wide fragmentation fringe.

Somewhat ironically, the loss of the second front tire made it easier for Rick to keep the truck moving in a more or less straight line, although the rapidly collapsing tire created much more drag. Since he had the accelerator floored, though, the truck kept on moving backwards until he judged them to be out of the line of fire.

"Sniper somewhere around the bend," said Vivian over the radio. "Went for the front tires first, then the windshield. Good shot too: three hits out of four rounds!"

"Can you judge the direction?" I asked.

There was a pause while Vivian and Rick consulted. "When the first shot came, we were pointed toward the headframe and the south end of the warehouses and mechanical shops. Rick thinks the round that came through the windshield was angled sharply down because the slug dropped right down in front of the dashboard, so the shooter may be on a rooftop or even the headframe itself."

At this point, both trucks had stopped and Don and I had run up to speak to Vivian and Rick. Don and I had brought a pair of binoculars with us from the houseboat so, after a brief conference, we decided to try an experiment. Taking one of the handheld radios, and having left Silver with stern instructions to remain with Don, I crept through some low bushes that had grown up around the edge of the flooded pit, and then switched to a crawl, with my chest on the ground and using my arms and elbows to slither and shuffle forward until I had a clear view of the mine's headframe and the warehouse and mechanical shop buildings. Then I stopped and radioed back. "I'm in position, go ahead."

At that point, Rick put his truck into the lowest forward gear and started forward, while Don in his truck followed immediately behind. This time, however, before rounding the bend in the road by the pit, Vivian opened the passenger-side door and jumped out, then Rick slipped over to the passenger side and jumped out as well. When he saw Rick jump, Don closed the distance between the two trucks, hit the gas and turned the steering wheel hard right. When Don's truck hit Rick's, it struck the passenger-side corner of the bumper, forcing Rick's truck to turn left. With the latter still being actively pushed, it turned the corner and its front end came into the view of the shooter.

Four more shots rang out in fairly rapid succession.

"Semi-automatic; could be a hunting rifle," said Rick, who had jumped onto the passenger-side running board of Don's truck when the latter had stopped and then reversed again at the sound of the first of the latest volley of shots. Vivian had taken the opportunity to jump into the box of Don's truck at the same time. "I heard another crack," continued Rick. "I think he put another round through the windshield of what's left of our truck."

"The shooter is up high in the headframe," I reported over the radio. "Must have a scope, because I saw some reflections."

"Rick and Don think it must be Delorme," said Vivian, who had retained her radio. "Rick figures he must have seen the two of us take the truck and become suspicious, but he may be unaware that you and Don are here."

"Your truck has stopped moving and it's gone quiet," I said, "I think it just stalled. I'll stay put and see if he comes out for a look."

"Roger," replied Vivian.

Nothing happened for what seemed like a very long time, but was probably not more than ten minutes. Then I saw a truck emerge from between the headframe and the other buildings.

"Truck emerging from near the headframe," I reported. "You might want to back up so you're out of sight if the shooter goes to investigate Rick's truck."

There was a pause, then "We agree. Reversing now."

With what I assumed was the shooter's truck coming straight towards me, it seemed safest for me to stay put and trust in the bushes to keep me hidden, although I'll admit to taking my gun out – just in case.

As it turned out, I needn't have worried because the truck turned left and went around the mechanical shops. I doubted the driver could hear my voice over the sounds from their truck at that point, so I got on the radio. "Truck has turned left, is ignoring Rick's truck, and heading west along the main road…. OK. It's passing the dining hall now and still heading west."

"We're coming around the south side of the pit now and will pick you up," said Vivian.

By that time, I'd changed position so I could better see down the length of the main road, although I still kept low to the ground to avoid being spotted in the truck's rear-view mirror.

By the time the truck carrying Don, Rick, Vivian, Silver, and the two guides rolled up to me, I was standing upright, still observing through the binoculars.

"Truck just took the branch road leading to the hospital before I lost sight of it," I said.

"They didn't bother to see if we were alive or dead!" said Vivian.

"Probably didn't care," put in Rick. "I still think it has to be Delorme. By now he knows Dexter's gone missing, he'll have guessed that Vivian and I have been working together, and he saw us following the two guides with the body. Even if we're still alive and uninjured, our truck's out of commission so he has time to report to the doctor and get a decision on whether to come search us out or make a run for it. Anyone disagree?"

None of us disagreed. A very short conference followed, with the result that Rick took over the remaining operational truck and he and Vivian dropped Don, Silver, and I off at the main dock where we'd moored our inflatable boat, then they drove off towards the hospital, with the two handcuffed guides still secured in the truck box.

Our plan, of course, was to split up. For one thing someone, probably Delorme, had a rifle and was a good shot, so we didn't want to be caught all together in one place. For another, we still didn't know whether the doctor would choose 'fight or flight' and, for the moment at least, the inflatable was our only other available transport. So, while Rick and Vivian drove the main road, Don, Silver, and I went in approximately the same direction but by water, aiming for the marina where there was a Twin Otter bush plane moored – the one that the charter pilot had told Rick and Don about eight days earlier. That plane was just the kind of thing that could be used for a quick getaway.

Our inflatable was roomy enough for our needs, and quite stable in choppy water, but whatever else it might be, it wasn't designed for speed, nor did it have a huge outboard motor on it. As a result, we were just rounding the bend in the shoreline by the former mine's tank farm when Vivian came on the radio.

"They didn't waste any time," she said. "By the time we reached the hospital, Delorme had already been there and he and doctor had left. We were just beginning to search for them when we heard the first engine start-up on that bush plane they have near the marina. We're driving to the marina now and have the plane in sight and – damn, I can see the second propellor beginning to turn. I don't think we're going to be able to stop them, but we'll see if we can grab a boat."

"Roger," I replied. "We have them in sight too. If we can get to the end of the breakwater in time, we may be able to block them in."

As we headed for the breakwater at full speed – which, as I've said, wasn't all that fast – we could see the plane begin to turn, driven by the one engine that was fully up to speed.

"This is going to be like playing chicken," yelled Don.

Soon, we were indeed pointed head-to-head and, as the second engine came up to speed the plane was clearly moving faster. Rather than the sedate pace at which a seaplane would normally taxi out from behind a breakwater, in this case the pilot had the plane moving as rapidly as possible.

"We're too small and light to stop them!" yelled Don. "We're going to have to hope they aren't willing to take the risk of ramming us and turn aside."

As we got closer and closer, however, the plane just kept on accelerating and it became clear that they were desperate enough to risk a collision. The only slight concession the pilot made was to turn the plane slightly to their starboard side in hopes they could squeeze between us and the end of the breakwater. I had just enough time to wonder whether the water there would be shallow enough to ground one of the floats when Don judged that we had gambled and lost, and threw the motor over in a hard turn to our starboard side.

The sight of the plane, with its twin roaring engines, bearing down on us was heart-stopping, and I had only enough time to reach for Silver's collar with one hand and a life-jacket with the other when the plane's port-side float hit us just back of the bow, causing our boat to flip over on its side, spilling everything into the water.

For the next few moments, I had thoughts only of getting my head above water and getting Silver supported by the life-jacket I'd grabbed, before he was lost to panic. For those of you that haven't followed all of our adventures, I should explain that Silver had a lifelong terror of being immersed in water due to a terrifying experience he'd had as a sled-dog when his whole team, dogs, sled, and musher, had broken through the ice when crossing a river, and all had been plunged into the icy water and nearly died[52]. Unfortunately, this wasn't even the first time Silver and Don and I had been rammed by something and sunk, although the previous time we'd been in a larger boat and had been rammed by a submarine[53], the experience from Silver's perspective must have been just about the same. In any case, when I surfaced, I still had a grip on both lifejacket and dog, and I was able to get the former underneath the latter, who had the instinct to dog paddle but I didn't like the look of terror in his eyes. Don had swum over to us by that time, and pulled us to the overturned inflatable so I could use one hand to hold the grab-rope that ran around the boat's perimeter.

From this vantage point, Don and I watched the next

developments play out. The bush plane had continued out into open water and was just beginning to turn into the wind when a speedboat came flying around the tip of the breakwater with Vivian at the helm and Rick looking over to see if we were OK. We could see, but not hear, him say something to Vivian who immediately cut the engine power, but when they saw us waving them forward, she pushed the throttle all the way forward and they accelerated away in pursuit of the bush plane.

"That doesn't look like one of their fishing boats," I said to Don.

"No. It's large and a lot more powerful. I think it must be for making trips over to Uranium City, or even for water skiing. I think she's going to catch them."

Indeed. While we watched, the speedboat was already approaching the plane when we heard its engines roar, as the pilot – presumably Delorme, I thought – began his takeoff run. In the speedboat, which was by this time on a parallel course and level with the plane's cockpit, I could see Rick waving at the pilot in an attempt to get him to abort. Then Rick abruptly sat back down and I thought he must have given up, but then suddenly he was standing again with his left hand holding on the windshield frame and his body twisting as if he was preparing to throw something.

"Oh my!" was all I had time to say before, with a convulsive jerk, we saw him throw something at the plane.

There was a sudden flash, followed by a brief but loud roar, after which the plane's left float seemed to suddenly disintegrate. *Rick had lighted and then thrown a stick of dynamite.* As that thought penetrated, we saw the plane sharply tip over on its port side. Then, when the wing tip hit the water, the drag on the wing and the momentum of the plane conspired to twist the plane even more sharply to port and then, listing at a steep angle, it began to settle in the water.

Still at the helm Vivian, for her part, had put the wheel over an instant after Rick had thrown the dynamite, which was not a moment too soon as the plane's wing tip very nearly hit the stern of their boat as they were turning away.

With the plane, still at a steep angle, wallowing in the waves, Vivian piloted the speedboat around to the plane's starboard side, where the front door had been thrown open and the doctor was struggling to get out. That he had to struggle in this was explained by the fact that he was using one arm to protectively cradle some kind of case that he held against his chest. Nevertheless, Rick was able to guide him safely into the speedboat.

As we later learned, in their haste to get away, neither Delorme nor the doctor had fastened their safety belts before taxiing out, so when the plane was so abruptly corkscrewed around and down in the water, both of them had been driven headfirst into the plane's windshield. The doctor, intact but bleeding heavily from a cut on his forehead, had insisted that Delorme was dead and that they should hasten to get away from the plane before it sank, carrying them with it but Rick, not believing him, left him in care of Vivian while he climbed into the plane himself to check.

Rick had found Delorme lying against the door, half in and half out of the water. He had been stunned by the impact of his head against the windshield and was just beginning to regain awareness of his surroundings when Rick reached over to help him get out. Once Rick and Delorme were safely in the speedboat, neither Rick nor Vivian said anything about the doctor's insistence on abandoning his assistant as they didn't want to set the two men to fighting with each other – yet – but Vivian made a mental note to use the episode to create a rift between the two when it came to getting statements from them later.

Abandoning the listing plane, Vivian next piloted the speedboat over to where we were. Since Don, Silver, and I were in no danger, and so very close to shore, Rick simply grabbed the inflatable's bow line, tied it to a cleat on the stern of their boat, and they slowly towed us back to the marina.

9 EPILOGUE

I arrested the bedraggled, but intact, Dr. Ernst Wildersbach and Ben Delorme, of course. The doctor was surprised to learn that Rick had been a plant, and he was stunned about Vivian. Delorme hadn't suspected Vivian but had always had a bad feeling about Rick.

The bag that the doctor had been so carefully clutching turned out to be a leather briefcase. It had opened up during his rescue, spilling out bundles of money. When we put the money back, we found that the briefcase had been packed full with cash in both Canadian and American currencies. I seized that as well, counted the money, and wrote him a receipt for it.

We asked the doctor about the dead person in the bundle, but he refused to say anything at all beyond demanding to see a lawyer.

Being about 25 kilometres (16 mi) away from Uranium City, our handheld radios were out of range, but the base station we had on the houseboat had more than enough range. So, leaving the others to watch our prisoners, Silver and I borrowed the speedboat so we could get to the houseboat, retrieve Dexter, and radio the Uranium City RCMP Detachment. With their help, we were able to put together enough boats to transfer the prisoners to the detachment where they could be held.

There were a number of subsequent investigations, of course, but I was only involved in the first one. The Uranium City Justice of the Peace issued a search warrant so we could go back and search the doctor's office and hospital for files related to the patients treated. The files we found showed that, in the eight months they had been operating the radiation-treatment machine, they had treated about eighty patients, most with multiple treatments. Of those, about one treatment in twenty malfunctioned and produced damaging radiation doses that quickly, or slowly, led to six patient deaths.

An attempt was made to recover the bodies from the flooded pit using grappling hooks which failed due to the repeated losses of the hooks, presumably due to their tendency to latch onto old machinery or timbers, some of which may have been disposed of from the surface when the mine closed. The second attempt, using commercial divers breathing specialized gas mixtures[54], was much more expensive but ultimately mostly successful. The divers were able to recover five bodies and reported seeing the other two, but the latter were too enmeshed in unstable-looking machinery to be safely recovered. Of the five bodies recovered, one was identified as being that of the senator and another that of the first CIA operative that had been using the name Johnson.

Ultimately, four of those that were recovered were sent to next of kin. The CIA refused to identify the operative known to us as Johnson, but Rick assured us that the body would be returned properly, if quietly, once it had been shipped to the U.S.

When it came to the trials, Wildersbach and Delorme pleaded not guilty to the various charges, but four of the other guides avoided stiff penalties by testifying against both of them. Given the guides' testimonies, Dexter's testimony regarding the computer-controlled aspects, the written records we found, and the bodies, Wildersbach was found guilty of practising medicine without a licence, operating the radiation treatment device without the required licenses and, of course, multiple offences related to the 'indignity or neglect of a dead body' section of the Criminal Code. It also turned out that Wildersbach was in the country illegally, although he wasn't to be deported until he had served his sentences in Canada. Delorme was found to be an accessory and sentenced accordingly.

As far as the original theft of the Amerior-8 machine and murder of the truck driver in Ontario, we suspected that the two men involved were probably Delorme and Wildersbach, with Delorme committing the murder, but the Ontario Provincial Police had been unable to find enough evidence to bring charges against anyone, and our own search of the hospital and residences at the Gunnar site hadn't produced any evidence linking the two men – or anyone else, for that matter – to those two particular crimes, and to this day they remain 'unsolved.'

Along the way, Accelerated Nuclear Inc. was notified of the discovery of their Amelior-8 machine, and also of Dexter's analysis and diagnosis regarding their faulty computer program. I didn't ever hear whether they went to the effort and expense of transporting the machine out, but they were so impressed with Dexter's work on the program that they offered him a full-time job at their headquarters in Mississauga, which he accepted. Although his advanced training, a standing, permanent-job offer, and a clean record should have been more than enough to get approved for a Canadian work permit, I like to think that recommendation letters from the RCMP, Canadian Forces, FBI, and CIA probably didn't hurt his chances either.

… Alex and Silver will return,
in "*An Investigative Mountie.*"

Laurie Schramm

SUMMARY

RCMP Sergeant Alex Houston, her dog-service partner Silver, and her husband Canadian Forces Major Don Harrison are sent on a covert mission with international implications. Someone has been using a fly-in-fishing camp on a remote northern lake as a cover for sophisticated, but unlicensed and highly secret cancer treatments thereby enabling wealthy patients – mostly from other countries - to avoid long waiting lists and get treated promptly. When a powerful U.S. Senator goes there for treatment and never returns, the CIA sends a covert operative to investigate. The alarm bells really go off when a charter pilot phones an unlisted CIA number to relay a codeword meaning that the operative had been captured or killed, at which point the U.S. Government reluctantly decides to formally ask for the Canadian Government's assistance.

ABOUT THE AUTHOR

Laurie Schramm comes from an RCMP family, grew up while living in the RCMP Barracks (Depot Division) in Regina, Saskatchewan, and spent several summers working as a civilian for the RCMP while in high school and university. Early personal influences included not only the real-life RCMP culture but also Hollywood's versions via such classics as *Rose Marie*, and *Susannah of the Mounties*. Many of the events described in this novel are based on the author's real life, although not necessarily within an RCMP context.

For more information, see Laurier L. Schramm on **Linked** in

and:

www.laurieschramm.ca

Laurie Schramm

ENDNOTES

1. In the early 1950s, a combination of cold-war security concerns and industrial technological advances led to uranium exploration in northern Saskatchewan, among other places, leading to several good quality discoveries. One of these, the Gunnar uranium deposit was discovered at the southern tip of the Crackingstone Peninsula on the northern shore of Lake Athabasca in 1952. Gunnar was considered to be the richest uranium strike in Canada at the time, and was unique in the region because it could be initially developed with a low-cost open-pit mine, as opposed to an underground mine which, in Gunnar's case, was developed later. Located about 40 km away from Uranium City, the site was considered to be too far away for routine services, so the company built a mill and a dedicated community in addition to the mines. When the Gunnar mill construction was completed in the fall of 1955 it doubled Canada's uranium production capacity. In 1956 the Gunnar mine was the largest uranium producer in the world. By the end of 1963, Gunnar's reserves were gone and the entire operation was simply shut-down. By this time Canada, the U.K. and the U.S. had more than enough uranium for their needs, and almost all of the other nearby mines were closed as well, leaving the entire Uranium City area to fall into decline.

2. In real life, and in the mid-1970s, Atomic Energy of Canada Limited (AECL) developed a very similar machine called

Therac-25 that inspired this part of the story. Costing a million dollars each, at the time, the Therac-25 was a compact, medical linear-accelerator, controlled by a PDP-11 computer, that could deliver either X-ray photons at 25 MeV or electrons at various energy levels.

3. In the real-life inspiration for this story, eleven Therac-25s were installed in North America for which six accidents causing serious injury and/or death occurred between 1985 and 1987, after which the machines were recalled to make extensive design changes that included hardware safeguards against software errors. See: N. Leveson, "Medical Devices: The Therac-25," in *Safeware: System Safety and Computers*, Addison-Wesley, 1995.

4. 'Langley' refers to a community in Fairfax County, Virginia, that is home to the headquarters of the U.S. Central Intelligence Agency.

5. Prime Minister's Office.

6. In the 1960s and '70s, according to investigative journalist Edward J. Epstein, "Mutual suspicion between the CIA and FBI of each other's moles and sources became so intense that in 1971 [FBI Director] Hoover broke off relations with the agency." The CIA's preoccupation with moles, traitors, and compromised sources eased later, in the 1980s, when much of the agency's focus shifted to electronic-intelligence gathering which, at the time, was judged to be secure. See E.J. Epstein, "Deception. The Once and Future Cold War," G.B. Putnam, N.Y., 1989 and "The War of the Moles," *New York Magazine*, 13 March 1978, pp. 12-13, https://www.cia.gov/readingroom/docs/CIA-RDP81M00980R002000090048-9.pdf

7. Ernesto 'Che' Guevara was a Marxist revolutionary and guerrilla leader in the Cuban Revolution against the dictator Batista in the 1950s. In later years, and especially after his death in 1965, his visage became a common countercultural symbol of rebellion.

8. During the Cold War, both the Soviet Union and the United States conducted extensive research programs into possible existence of, and possible military uses of ESP. See for example: A. Jacobsen, *Phenomena: The Secret History of the U.S. Government's Investigations into Extrasensory Perception and*

Psychokinesis, Back Bay Books, Boston, 2018; and Martin Ebon, *Psychic Warfare: Threat or Illusion?* McGraw-Hill, NY, 1983.

9. See *An Inconvenient Mountie*, ISBN: 978-1-9994940-0-1.

10. The Canadian Police Information Centre (CPIC) is Canada's national police database. When the author worked at CPIC in 1971 (before its launch), we referred to it by spelling out the acronym's letters – 'C-P-I-C' - but after the system became operational in 1972, people in the field began to refer to it as 'seapick.' See: B. Sharp, *"Cop,"* Friesen Press, Victoria, BC, 2014.

11. At the time of this story, medical linear accelerators were just beginning to become widely available. In 1976, for example, there were only about 336 in operation worldwide. See: S.G. Laskar *et al.*, "Access to Radiation Therapy: From Local to Global and Equality to Equity," *JCO Global Oncology*, **2022**, *8(August 12)*, 7 pp., doi.org/10.1200/GO.21.00358

12. The de Havilland DHC-6 Twin Otter is a twin-engine, short-takeoff and landing aircraft developed in the 1960s and still in production (now by Viking Air). Easily switched from wheeled-, to float- or ski landing gear, they are ubiquitous in Canada's more northern and remote regions and one of the most famous of Canada's 'bush planes.'

13. On a merchant ship, these are usually the First Watch (20:00–24:00), Middle Watch (00:00–04:00), Morning Watch (04:00–08:00), Forenoon Watch (08:00–12:00), Afternoon Watch (12:00–16:00), and Dog Watch (16:00–20:00).

14. Ripstop nylon contains crosshatched coarse, strong, yarns at intervals so that tears will not spread, and is often coated to make it water resistant or waterproof. It originated during the Second World War, some time after nylon was adopted as a replacement for silk in parachutes. Ripstop nylon began appearing in consumer products for campers and hikers in 1980, and would still have been regarded as state-of-the-art at the time of this story.

15. The largest known lake trout, at 102 lb. (46 kg), was caught in a gill net in Lake Athabasca in 1961. There is a photo of it in the article at: BCLSS, "Lake Trout (Salvelinus namaycush)," BCLSS Newsletter, 13(1) April, 2010, BC Lake Stewardship

Society, https://www.bclss.org/news/lake-
trout#:~:text=The%20largest%20known%20lake%20trout,)%20(Mathias%2
C%202009).

16. The headframe is a tall structure that sits directly above the main shaft of an underground mine and contains the hoisting mechanisms for raising and lowering miners, mining equipment, supplies, waste rock, and the mined ore.

17. Generally termed the Norwalk virus at the time of this story, this common cause of gastroenteritis was renamed norovirus in 2002.

18. PP796 is a triazolo-pyridine compound discovered by ICI Pharmaceuticals in the early 1970s. Originally intended to be used in the treatment of asthma, it was found to have a strong emetic effect in humans. A dose of 5-8 mg causes nausea and induces vomiting, accompanied by dizziness and sweating and flushing. At this dosage, vomiting occurs within 30 mins. The half-life in humans following single oral doses is between 1.5 and 3.5 hours. Due to its strong emetic effect, PP796 has been included in formulations of the herbicide paraquat, most commonly Gramoxone™, since 1976. It is included as a safety measure because paraquat is highly toxic to humans, the idea being that if a person accidently ingests the formulation, the PP796 component will cause them to almost immediately vomit. Although paraquat was banned in 2007 by the European Union, formulations of it are still widely used in about 100 other countries (but not Canada since 2023).

19. The ubiquitous amber-coloured plastic containers for prescription medications came into widespread use in the early 1970s. The amber-coloured plastic blocks UV light that would otherwise potentially degrade the medication.

20. Limnological research focuses on inland water systems, such as streams, rivers, and lakes. It can involve any or all of the physics, chemistry, and biology of these water bodies.

21. See *An Indestructible Mountie*, ISBN: 978-1-9994940-4-9.

22. Stereo microscopes have binocular eyepieces and produce a 3D (stereo) image at relatively low magnifications, such as 10X to 40X. They are usually set-up to provide reflected-light illumination, but some can be used in transmitted-light mode. Compound microscopes commonly have either single- or binocular eyepieces and produce high- to very high

magnifications of small samples placed on a microscope slide. They can be used in reflected or transmitted light modes, sometimes using illumination of wavelengths outside of the visible light range, and typically produce magnifications in the range 40X to 1,000X.

23. The Digital Voice Protection (DVP) algorithm for the encryption/decryption of voice communications was developed by Motorola in the mid-1970s (it is also known as VULCAN, Motorola's internal codename).

24. It wasn't until 1984 that municipalities in Alberta were able to allow, or continue to prohibit, retail stores opening on Sundays.

25. Although CFB Edmonton is close to the city of Edmonton, it is also just south of the hamlet of Namao and was formerly called RCAF Station Namao. For many years, the base continued to be referred to by its older, short-form name: Namao.

26. The Cessna 206 is a single-engine, six-seat, aircraft with fixed landing gear that can be equipped with floats, amphibious floats, or skis, used in commercial air service as well as for personal use. It has been a popular choice as a bush plane, among other things, since its introduction in 1962 and it was still in production at the time of writing.

27. At 7,850 km² (3,030 sq mi), Lake Athabasca is the 20th largest lake in the world by surface area. In terms of lakes within, or bordered by Canada, only the Great Lakes, Great Bear Lake, and Lake Winnipeg are larger.

28. The Athabasca sand dunes extend for about 100 kilometres (60 mi) along the southern edge of Lake Athabasca and represent one of the most northerly active sand dune formations on Earth. Some of the individual sand dunes are as much as 1,500 metres long and as tall as 30 metres.

29. Canadian Hydrographic Service chart CHS6310.

30. Zodiac inflatable boats became famous in the 1960s and '70s due to their ubiquitous appearance in the underwater documentaries made by the French oceanographer and filmmaker Jacques Cousteau (who also co-invented the first successful open-circuit SCUBA breathing apparatus). The inflatable tubes in Zodiac boats, and their similarly-designed competitors, were made of synthetic rubber compounds, one

of which was DuPont Hypalon®. In addition to being strong and flexible, these materials have very good resistance to heat, ultraviolet light, and gasoline. Dupont stopped making the Hypalon material in 2010.

31. See *An Inconspicuous Mountie* 978-1-9994940-2-5.

32. Ignoring the radioisotopes with half-lives of less than 22 years, the uranium decay series is: uranium-238 → uranium-234 → thorium-230 → radium-226 → lead-210 → lead-206 (which is stable).

33. In real life, the movement of mine tailings into Langley Bay (adjacent to the Gunnar mine and mill site) really has led to high radionuclide concentrations in the resident whitefish and, to a lesser extent, the pike. See, for example: D.T. Waite, *et al.,* "The Effect of Uranium Mine Tailings on Radionuclide Concentrations in Langley Bay, Saskatchewan, Canada," *Arch. Environ. Contam. Toxicol.,* **1988**, *17*, 373-380.

34. In real life, they are. At the time of writing, radionuclide levels in the flesh and bone of fish caught in the flooded Gunnar open-mine pit are one to two orders of magnitude greater than levels in fish caught from an uncontaminated area of Lake Athabasca. The fish have been accumulating the radionuclides from materials being mobilized in and/or washed into the pit.

35. In real life, the Gunnar open-pit mine was mined to a final depth of 328 feet (110 m) below the level of the lake.

36. When active, the mined uranium had been crushed and processed using an acid-leach process for which the sulphuric acid needed was produced on-site from sulphur that was barged in from Alberta. For more details see: L.L. Schramm, *Gunnar Uranium Mine. Canada's Cold War Ghost Town,* Amazon.com Inc., 2016, ISBN: 978-0-9958081-2-6.

37. 'Check your six' was originally an Air Force term for 'watch out behind you,' based on looking for enemy aircraft to the rear at the 6 O'clock position. It was later broadened to other services, and broader meanings (including off-duty situations).

38. Forcite was a 'gelatin dynamite,' comprising 30 to 80% nitroglycerin mixed with cellulose, sodium or potassium nitrate, and a hydrocarbon like tar (to make it waterproof). It was commonly used in mining operations up until about the end of the 1970s.

39. At the time of this story, the printer would likely have been

something like the DECwriter III, capable of printing 180 characters per second in draft mode; about 300 lines per minute on 9⅞" paper.

40. The relative popularities and meaning of the terms nerd and geek have changed over the decades. Those characterized as nerds or geeks have stereotypically been male, intelligent, socially awkward, and dedicated to the point of obsession with a specific field or topic. In general, where a distinction is made, it is that geeks are fans and students of their subjects whereas nerds are practitioners of them.

41. Black Sabbath, although already a hit in the 1970s, was one of the top heavy-metal rock groups in the 1980s. Their anti-war song *War Pigs* (1970) is often cited as the best of their many hits.

42. See: S. Cheryan *et al.*, "The Stereotypical Computer Scientist: Gendered Media Representations as a Barrier to Inclusion for Women," *Sex Roles*, **2013**, *69*, 58–71.

43. Originally, the term computer hacker referred to the early computer nerds, for whom the term 'hack' was applied to neat hardware or programming tricks; but it later changed to the modern meaning of someone that acts to subvert computer security.

44. Wide Area Telephone Service (WATS) was a flat-rate, long-distance telephone service plan for businesses in North America, by which they were given a special number and an included number of hours. WATS was introduced in 1961 and operated until the early 1980s.

45. For a real-life example, see: S. Levy, *Hackers: Heroes of the Computer Revolution*, Anchor Press/Doubleday, N.Y., 1984.

46. This kind of thing actually happened to several patients in the real-life Therac-25 case. See N.G. Leveson and C.S. Turner, "An Investigation of the Therac-25 Accidents," *Computer*, **1993**, *26(7)*, 18-41.

47. The Stanford Artificial Intelligence Lab (SAIL) at Stanford University, sometimes called the 'AI Lab,' was founded in 1965, it was merged into Stanford's Computer Science Department in 1980, but then re-emerged as a stand-alone in 2004.

48. 'Standby to standby,' like 'hurry up and wait,' is military

sarcasm referring either to having to wait for long periods of time because of logistics or command indecisiveness, or to the military's tendency to perform tasks quickly and then be idle.

49. At 59°23' N, Alex would only have been about 795 km (500 mi) south of the Arctic Circle.

50. Twilight is caused by the scattering of the sun's light in the upper atmosphere despite the fact that the sun's geometric centre lies below the horizon. At Alex's location and time of year, the twilight sequence would have been approximately as follows: civil twilight (21:30-22:20; sun's centre 0-6° below the horizon), nautical twilight (22:20-23:50; sun's centre 6-12° below the horizon), astronomical twilight (23:50-02:50; sun's centre 12-18° below the horizon), nautical twilight (02:50-04:20), civil twilight (04:20-05:20), and sunrise at about 05:20.

51. At the time of this story, the Eldorado uranium mine was still in full operation, and Uranium City had a six-person RCMP Detachment, but it didn't last much longer. The Eldorado mine, among others in the area, closed in 1982, causing an economic collapse that forced most residents of the community to leave. See: "Dennis Lars Schneider," *Pillars of the Force*, Friends of the RCMP Heritage Centre, Regina, SK, accessed 26 July 2024, https://mpvirtualpillars.ca/listing/auto-draft/

52. See *An International Mountie*, ISBN 978-1-9994940-6-3.

53. See *An Indestructible Mountie*, ISBN 978-1-9994940-4-9.

54. Although fictional, this would have been technically feasible as commercial divers can perform very deep dives breathing gas mixtures such as Heliox (a mixture of oxygen and helium, but no nitrogen) and a rebreather (which provides mobility by avoiding the need for surface-fed hoses). A diver with a Heliox rebreather would be able to operate at the maximum depth of the pit, which is about 110 m (360 ft).

ADVENTURES OF THE FIRST WOMAN MOUNTIE

www.laurieschramm.ca

Laurie Schramm

Adventures of the First
Woman Mountie

Laurie Schramm